ALAN
SHATTER
LAURA

ALAN SHATTER
LAURA

POOLBEG

First Published 1989

This edition published 2013
by Poolbeg Press Ltd.
123 Grange Hill, Baldoyle,
Dublin 13, Ireland
Email: poolbeg@poolbeg.com

A catalogue record for this book is available from the British Library.

ISBN 978-1-84223-608-6

Cover design by Steven Hope
Typeset by Patricia Hope in Sabon 11.2/15
Printed and bound by CPI Group Ltd., Croydon, CRO 4YY

www.poolbeg.com

Note on the Author

Alan Shatter is presently Minister for Justice, Equality and Defence in the Irish government. He was first elected to the Dáil (the Irish parliament) in 1981. He was for many years a partner in the law firm Gallagher Shatter and he specialised in family law. Prior to his appointment to government in March 2011, he was a regular advocate before the Irish courts and appeared in a number of seminal cases, including some in the area of adoption. He is a well-known advocate and campaigner for legal and social reform. Alan and his wife Carol have a son Dylan and a daughter Kelly. He has published a number of academic works on Irish family law. Both prior to and since his appointment to government, he has pioneered and published an unprecedented number of reforming laws. *Laura* is his first novel.

To Carol, Dylan and Kelly

one

The realisation suddenly struck her. Too much time had passed and she now knew for certain that it was not going to happen. She had visited countless specialists and had on six occasions been admitted to hospital for exploratory tests. The doctors had all said that they could give no explanation for her failure to become pregnant. Everything would be alright. It would happen eventually. They had been wrong. It had not happened. Drugs had not helped and IVF had not worked. They had been married for just over eight years and still she was not pregnant. Jenny Masterson was now convinced that she never would be.

Once, long before, they discussed the possibility of adoption but had not really considered it a serious option. There was always a presumption that the problem, whatever it was, would be solved – that she would eventually become pregnant. Every day Jenny dreamed about how she would break the good news to

John. She would wait until her period was three weeks late before having a pregnancy test carried out. When it proved positive, she would tell him over a candlelit dinner. He would be ecstatic and sweep her into his arms and they would make passionate love that night. It had remained a dream.

In the eyes of the outside world they had everything: a beautiful detached house perched on the side of a mountain overlooking Dublin with the city spread out like a mat below them, a successful business, two cars, two continental holidays each year, and a dog. Weekends they spent in their country cottage in Ashford, Co. Wicklow. They danced, played tennis, regularly visited their relatives and got on well with everyone who came into contact with them. They both hated cocktail parties and other big social gatherings but enjoyed quiet meals out with friends.

They were unaffected by the seven-year itch. Jenny knew that she was attractive with her fair colouring and petite build and she enjoyed the occasional flirtation. This reassured her of her femininity and desirability but she never permitted it to go further. She loved John and he loved her. Throughout their marriage they had remained true to each other.

They were both very fond of children. Jenny's sister Ruth had two children: Declan, aged five, and Susan, aged three, whom they saw regularly. She and John loved them dearly and at times Jenny felt that they loved them too dearly. They were not their own but they treated them as if they were. She frequently bought clothes for

Susan and Declan. John never missed an opportunity to buy them toys. The children often spent the weekend with them in their cottage in Ashford, as did Ruth and her husband, David. Jenny now realised that she and John had become weekend parents to them. If they did not visit, they both missed them terribly. Missed the children, not her sister or brother-in-law.

John and Jenny rarely quarrelled but one subject caused tension and after a while they developed the habit of avoiding discussing it altogether. Although they accompanied each other on visits to specialists and discussed their "problem" on such visits, they never broached it when they were alone. A barrier had been erected. It was as if they had tacitly acknowledged that to discuss their difficulty when alone together would be an admission of failure – an admission that Jenny would never conceive, that they would never have their own child.

Twice in the past year they had discussed adoption, not as a possible option for themselves but in relation to a couple with whom they were friendly and who had just successfully completed the process.

Jenny's mother brought up the same topic on one of her visits.

"I see Kate and Arthur have adopted a beautiful baby boy," she said, in the deceptively casual tone of one who is pretending merely to be passing on a piece of news. When Jenny said nothing and kept her head bent over the dishwasher she was stacking, her mother continued: "I suppose it was inevitable that they would adopt. After all, they have been married for almost ten years now and have no children of their own."

"I suppose so," agreed Jenny, recognising her mother's comments as the fishing exercise intended and quickly passing on to another subject.

Although she had avoided discussing it, the idea of adoption took root in Jenny's mind. John was thirty-four and she was twenty-nine and she knew that adoption societies favoured fairly young parents. John was an only child and his parents had both died when he was still a teenager. Jenny knew how much he wanted a family of his own and feared that if they continued to side-step the issue the passage of time would make adoption more difficult. She had not planned how she would suggest it to John; she had not even finally decided to bring up the subject. One night over dinner it just came out.

"I think we should adopt," she whispered.

"Sorry, what did you say?" John asked.

"I think we should adopt," she repeated, still hesitantly but much more loudly, uncertain and fearful of his response.

"So do I," he replied, looking straight into her eyes.

Jenny was startled by the rapidity of his reply. She realised that she had been subconsciously preparing herself for arguments, tears, wounded pride and possible rejection. At last she had plucked up the courage to make the suggestion and within minutes everything was agreed.

"I have been thinking about adoption for weeks now," he explained, "but I have never felt strong enough to raise the subject. I was somehow afraid of your reaction. Afraid you would hate me for suggesting it after all you have gone through. Yes, I agree, we should adopt."

He knew how much she wanted to become pregnant and understood the emotional distance she had to travel to face the reality of adoption. It really meant that she was finally accepting that she would never give birth to a baby of her own. He had been reluctant to force the issue, always feeling she would eventually get there in her own time and not wishing to hurry the process. For a few moments they just sat quietly looking lovingly at each other.

Then John silently stood up and went to the kitchen. For over a year a bottle of champagne had lain at the back of the fridge, left over from some family celebration. The cork popped and they sat quietly at the table sipping the champagne out of long-stemmed glasses. They held hands across the top of the table and said nothing.

The bottle emptied and the champagne finished, he carried her up the stairs into the bedroom, realising that they were both slightly drunk. She lay beneath him on the bed, its soft mattress rising and falling as their bodies joined together in a passionate celebration of the decision they had made. Breathless and exhausted, Jenny closed her eyes and drifted off to sleep. Unseen in the darkened room, a smile came to her lips, reflecting her subconscious thoughts. A part, at least, of Jenny's dream had been fulfilled.

two

Jenny sat in a dark waiting room in a nineteenth-century building in Sackville Road at the back of Dublin's O'Connell Street. St Mark's Adoption Society had been originally formed in 1910, but had not officially become an adoption society until 1953, just after adoption had become legal in Ireland. Before that it had been run exclusively by a religious order. Founded as a Roman Catholic institution to provide a home for orphaned and abandoned Catholic children, in the early 1920s it had started placing such children with childless Catholic families. In those days the children were officially placed as foster children although it was adoption in everything but name. Originally, the main aim of St Mark's was to ensure that Catholic children preserved their religious faith and were not proselytised by any protestant organisation. By the 1960s it had become exclusively an adoption agency, and although a priest was head of the society most of its workers were non-religious, mainly female, social workers.

Jenny sat in the waiting room for over half an hour, her anxiety increasing with each passing minute. The magazines on the waiting-room table were old and as tattered as the building itself and failed to retain her interest. She wondered how many hopeful adopters before her had sat on the same dilapidated armchair waiting nervously to be called. The room seemed to close in on her and she had a strong desire to run away, back out into the street. Then she heard her name being called.

"Mrs Masterson, Mrs Masterson! Mrs Gavin can see you now."

Jenny started, then recognised the voice of the grey-haired receptionist who had shown her into the waiting room.

Jenny passed into a small but cheerfully decorated office. A woman, whom she presumed to be Mrs Gavin, met her as she entered and indicated with an out-stretched arm that she should sit in an armchair on the other side of her desk. The social worker looked as if she was in her mid-thirties. Although she was trying to be chatty and informal to put Jenny at her ease, her approach only succeeded in making her feel more tense and nervous.

Mrs Gavin noted down Jenny's name, her husband's name and their address.

"Why have you made an appointment to see someone in St Mark's?" she enquired.

"We – my husband, John and I – wish to adopt a child," Jenny replied, taken aback and wondering what other explanation the woman could expect from someone who had made an appointment for an interview with an adoption agency.

"I see," said Mrs Gavin. "And why do you want to adopt?"

The interview lasted an hour and a half. After twenty minutes or so Jenny felt the tension lifting and she spoke freely and easily. She described her relationship with John, their desire to have children, her medical history and their attachment to her sister's children. The social worker noted the names and addresses of the doctors they had attended and sought her permission to write to them for medical reports. She asked questions about their home, about John's work and about her own occupation. Jenny explained that she kept herself busy working from home as a secretary and that John was the owner and managing director of an advertising and public relations company in Dublin.

"I'll need to call to your home to meet both of you and discuss your application in more detail," Mrs Gavin said. "How about Thursday the fifteenth?" she asked as she consulted a diary on her desk. "That's the earliest I can manage, ten days from now." Her pen was poised over the page. "What time would suit you best? I imagine it will have to be evening if your husband works normal hours."

"That's fine," said Jenny. "How about eight o'clock?"

Mrs Gavin made a note of their address in her appointment book and explained to Jenny that a report would have to be prepared for a meeting of the society.

"This is standard procedure. A decision will be made as to you and your husband's suitability as adoptive parents and once you are approved, your names will be added to the society's list of applicants. Now, is there anything you want to know?"

"I don't think so," replied Jenny, smiling with relief that the initial interview was coming to an end.

A few moments later, Mrs Gavin shook Jenny's hand warmly and showed her out.

As Jenny drove home she thought the meeting had gone well. She expected that Mrs Gavin was used to people being tense at the first interview and was reassured by the woman's friendliness; it had seemed merely professional to her at the start of the interview but genuine enough by the time their discussions had concluded. Filled with hope, over supper that evening she told John how the interview had gone.

* * *

On the appointed evening, Mrs Gavin arrived punctually and stayed for two hours. Jenny quickly realised that she was asking John many of the same questions she herself had been asked and was relieved when he gave similar replies. While Jenny made tea, John showed Mrs Gavin around their house and introduced her to Rebel, their dog. The evening went well.

Mrs Gavin visited on two further occasions, on one of these bringing along a Mrs Comerford, who was introduced to them as another social worker from the society.

Two months after Jenny's first visit to St Mark's, a letter arrived. John was sitting at breakfast when Jenny, opening the post in the hall, recognised the St Mark's motif on the top of the page she pulled from the envelope. She rushed into the kitchen so that they could read it together, hoping for the best, fearing the worst.

"*You have been formally approved*," the letter said, "*as adoptive applicants. Your names have been inserted in the society's register of prospective adopters.*"

Their elation lasted for about three months. During this time John and Jenny told Jenny's parents – the prospective grandparents – that they had been approved for adoption and made plans for the baby's arrival. They wondered whether it would be a boy or a girl. Mrs Gavin had asked them whether they had a preference and both of them had automatically replied that they did not mind in the least. The Mastersons turned John's old study into a bedroom for the baby and chose yellow wallpaper with brown teddy-bears.

"Suitable for either a boy or a girl. That's right," Jenny's mother had said approvingly on one of her frequent visits. Jenny had never felt closer to her mother. It was almost as if she were pregnant and the two women were sharing the joy of expectation.

A cot, baby blankets, sheets and a mobile were bought. Jenny discussed with her sister the relative advantages and disadvantages of different brands of disposable nappies and came down in favour of one of them. Night after night John and Jenny discussed boys' and girls' names. Eventually they agreed on a shortlist of four names, two of each – Niall or David for a boy and Laura or Siobhán for a girl.

They discussed possible schools, sports they would like their child to play and wondered whether the baby would possess any unusual skills. Most of all they wondered what the baby would look like.

But as the waiting period extended beyond a year, John and Jenny became anxious, especially when relatives asked them whether they had any news. They did not wish to pester the adoption society. Although they discussed the possibility of contacting Mrs Gavin, they agreed they would not do so in case they betrayed their anxiety to her and, by so doing, in some way jeopardise their chance to adopt. They felt dependent on the society, grateful to it for accepting them but also afraid of it, in case something they did or said changed that acceptance to rejection.

Halfway through the thirteenth month, John made an appointment to see Mrs Gavin without telling Jenny. Perhaps there was an administrative error, perhaps some secretary had forgotten to enter their name on the society's register. Perhaps the society had changed its mind and Mrs Gavin was afraid to break the news to them. It was mid-January and John was determined to discover what was wrong before another month had passed.

Sitting down in Mrs Gavin's room, John was momentarily at a loss for words, simply not knowing how to begin. He did not have to.

"What a wonderful coincidence! I'm delighted you came in to see me today, John," she said. "I have good news. We have a baby for you. A little girl, born five days ago. I was going to visit you both this evening to tell you."

He sat there, stunned, and realised that he was grinning stupidly at her. She went on talking.

"I'm sorry that you have had to wait so long. Fewer children are being placed for adoption with us these days. So many unmarried mothers are keeping their children and bringing them up themselves, you know."

"We were a little worried about the delay," he admitted cautiously.

"The baby is still in the maternity hospital but she will be released tomorrow. Her mother has already signed a placement agreement allowing us to place her baby with adopters and I would like you and Jenny to come in tomorrow at three o'clock to collect the baby."

John later had no recollection of his drive home from the society. The car seemed to possess a life of its own, stopping when traffic lights changed to red, moving when they changed to green. It parked in the driveway and let him out. He knew Jenny would be there, anticipated her joy as he opened the front door and moved down the hallway, floating, not walking.

"Darling, is that you?" she shouted from the kitchen.

For a moment he was unable to speak. Then, bursting into the kitchen, he shouted, "We've got a baby, a baby girl! The society want us to collect her tomorrow."

Jenny turned around, staring at him with her mouth open. But no words came. Standing in the kitchen, arms wrapped tightly around each other, they sobbed with joy.

* * *

Jenny lay awake for most of the night, resisting the temptation to interrupt John's snoring and awaken him. She tried again to imagine what their daughter would look like. The colour of her eyes and hair. The shape of her face. She was curious about the mother. Who was she? How old was she? What did she work at? Why had she chosen to give up her baby?

The thought of the father also intrigued her. Who was he? For how long had he known the mother? Was he in love with her, or had he abandoned her? Did he know his daughter was being adopted? Jenny knew that if she had become pregnant while unmarried, she could not have given her baby away to another woman, no matter how difficult the circumstances. She could not understand how a mother could do so when she had carried a child in her womb for nine months. How could she hand over to someone else the life she had felt moving and kicking inside her, that had grown within her and been a part of her?

Jenny felt both grateful to the child's mother and envious of her. She was grateful for being given an opportunity to become a real parent, a mother with a child of her own, but she was also envious of this woman's ability to conceive. Jenny ached to experience pregnancy, the kicks, contractions, the dash to the hospital and the release and joy of childbirth. It was an intense and mysterious mixture of pleasure and pain that she would never know.

She had watched her sister breastfeeding Declan and Susan and had always imagined herself like that with her own baby. Once, when baby-sitting, she had put Susan to her breast and had allowed her to suck at her nipple. As Susan frantically sucked, she could see the frustration build up on the child's face until she pushed Jenny away, red in the face and screaming for food. Jenny had felt so inadequate at that moment and, lying awake now, she felt inadequate again. Because she had not given birth, she would be unable to breastfeed her daughter. She was surprised that she had not realised this earlier. John and she had thought of everything else but not this. For some reason they had both presumed that she would breastfeed the baby as her sister had done.

The next day, before John came home to collect her so that they could drive to St Mark's together, Jenny went shopping. She bought four baby bottles, four teats, a bottle-warmer, a sterilising unit and a bottle of Milton.

* * *

As she sat with John waiting for Mrs Gavin, the room in St Mark's seemed more cheerful and less claustrophobic to Jenny than she remembered it from her first visit. Perhaps it was the sunshine streaming through the windows. Maybe it was just their elation.

Mrs Gavin invited them into her room. The baby would be brought in to them shortly, she explained. First she had to go over the various steps to be taken in completing the adoption process and give them some information about the baby's background. She explained that she would visit them a number of times during the following weeks to continue her assessment. When this was finished they could formally apply to the Adoption Authority for an adoption order. They would then be visited by the Authority's social worker and, six to eight months from then, all being well, an adoption order would be made.

The baby's biological mother had to sign a "final consent" form before the Adoption Authority could make their order and she could, in theory, reclaim her child at any time before the order was made, but this was not something that should cause them any worry. In her experience it had rarely caused any difficulties and on only one occasion in the previous ten years had a mother insisted on the return to her of a baby placed with adopters by St Mark's.

She handed them a two-page typed document containing information about the baby and read it through quickly with them. The baby had no abnormalities; she had been seven pounds seven ounces at birth; was developing well; no allergic history in the family on the mother's side; unknown on the father's side; BCG inoculation had been administered when the baby was four days old with no adverse reaction.

John and Jenny only partially heard Mrs Gavin. Her voice echoed around the room and, although she only talked for ten minutes, it felt much longer.

"I think that's everything," she concluded. "Is there anything either of you want me to clarify or repeat before we bring in your baby?"

"I don't think so," Jenny replied quietly, glancing at John. He nodded in agreement.

Mrs Gavin lifted the phone on her desk. "You can bring the baby in now," she said to an anonymous voice at the other end of the phone.

Within seconds the door opened and there stood the receptionist with a crying baby in her arms. Jenny instinctively reached up to take her and, as she did so, the baby miraculously stopped crying. As Jenny cradled her in her arms, John sat transfixed in his armchair staring at them both, his wife and his daughter – their first child.

three

They called her Laura. She had blue eyes and wispy light-blonde hair and she cried very little. Her main needs were simply to be fed and changed every four hours. Since she fed well from a bottle, Jenny's feeling of guilt at her inability to breastfeed quickly evaporated. John and Jenny rapidly settled into a routine, alternating between them the midnight and 4 a.m. feeds. Laura was so regular that John used to say he could set his watch by her. She would wake crying at five minutes to the hour and would fall asleep again forty-five minutes after waking. Seven weeks after her arrival she started to sleep on until between seven and eight in the morning and the tiredness caused by having to wake for the early morning feed was quickly forgotten.

Mrs Gavin continued to visit them regularly and, after a few weeks, to their relief, announced that

Laura had settled in well. She seemed pleased, more chatty and less formal than she had been in earlier meetings. The grandparents showered presents on Laura and their home seemed to have a never-ending stream of visiting relations and friends. It soon developed the distinct appearance of an overstocked toyshop.

Eight weeks after Laura's arrival they escaped from Dublin and took her to their cottage in Wicklow. For the first time the three of them were able to spend four days together, unvisited and uninterrupted by the outside world. They talked, shopped and walked by day and listened to music at night. Laura was fed, changed, played with and marvelled at. Lying quietly in her pram, sometimes awake, sometimes asleep, she was proudly introduced to the shop assistants in Wicklow town. Propped contentedly in Jenny's arms she sucked at her bottle in The Coffee Shop in Wicklow's main street as Jenny and John tucked into delicious hot scones and cups of Bewley's coffee.

As the weeks passed, they watched her grow and develop. Soon she was no longer just a baby but an individual with her own personality and her own likes and dislikes. Laura loved mashed banana but would spit out mashed carrot. She chewed her rubber duck and screamed if it was taken away from her but showed no interest in a large teddy-bear John had bought for her. She liked shoes and slippers. If they were left near her when she was lying on the floor, they would inevitably become playthings. When she was awake in her cot, she could lie quietly for over an hour if music was playing. As soon as the music stopped, she would scream.

Rebel, their Labrador dog, was suspicious of Laura at first, but by the start of the second month after her arrival had become so attached to her that during her waking periods he could not be separated from her. As she got bigger and more active, he would sit quietly in the corner of the lounge watching her roll and play, whimpering happily, his tail beating the carpet. Often when she rolled near him, she would poke his face or pull his hair but he never retaliated or showed any sign of annoyance. The rhythm of his tail would continue uninterrupted. He accompanied them on all their walks, marching by the side of her pram like a guard dog on patrol. In the mornings when Laura awoke he would rush into her bedroom with Jenny, push his tongue through the side of the cot and lick her feet. She would giggle with delight and Rebel's tail would sweep through the air. One night Jenny remarked to John that Rebel treated her almost as if she was his puppy rather than their child.

After Laura had been with them for two months the Mastersons filled in the official application form on Mrs Gavin's instructions, asking the Adoption Authority to make an adoption order. Seven weeks later they had their first visit from the Adoption Authority social worker.

The woman introduced herself as Imelda Hennessy. She had grey hair, looked to be in her late fifties, wore a neat blue jacket and skirt and completely unnerved Jenny when she called unexpectedly one morning.

"I'm from the Adoption Authority," she announced, as soon as Jenny opened the door.

"Come into the lounge," Jenny said, struggling hard to regain her composure.

She stayed for over an hour, asking Jenny many of the same questions Mrs Gavin had asked her and John many months earlier. She demanded, rather than asked, to be shown around the house and quizzed Jenny about Laura.

"Has she been sick at any stage since she was placed with you?" she enquired.

"She had a cold that lasted for a few days when she was nine weeks old," Jenny replied, "but nothing very much other than that."

"Has she suffered any bruising?"

Jenny, taken aback by the unexpected question, recalled that three days earlier, on the morning of Mrs Gavin's last visit, she had for a brief moment taken her eyes off Laura while she was rolling on the floor and Laura had banged her head on the side of a coffee table. A large lump immediately formed on her forehead and it had taken Jenny almost half an hour to pacify her. By the following day a large purple bruise, the remains of which were still visible, had replaced the swelling.

Imelda Hennessy listened impassively as Jenny

described what had happened. She continued to jot down notes as she had done throughout her visit, making no comment other than to ask Jenny whether Laura had been bruised on any other occasion.

"No," replied Jenny, trying to stay calm since she thought she saw disbelief registering on the other woman's face.

She was relieved when her visitor left and couldn't put the discussion with Imelda Hennessy out of her mind for the rest of the day, finding it impossible to concentrate on anything else.

"I think she suspects we are baby-batterers," she said anxiously to John that evening, as she described the morning's interview to him over dinner.

"I'm sure she doesn't," he replied, trying to put Jenny's mind at rest as he struggled to conceal his own anxiety, wondering what conclusions the woman had reached as a result of her interview.

They both tossed and turned in bed that night, neither giving voice to their thoughts but both fearing that something could go wrong. It was natural to presume after Laura had been placed with them that it was only a question of time before an adoption order would be made and that they merely had to go through the formalities. They saw Laura not as another woman's child but as their own daughter. It had never seriously occurred to either of them that a social worker could decide that they were unsuitable and want to take Laura from them.

Imelda Hennessy made three further visits, all in

the evening, all by appointment. Each visit was an ordeal. She was always formal, questioning, never reassuring. Neither of them liked her and they suspected she did not like them.

At each interview she asked about Laura's health, whether she had been involved in any accidents since her last visit, whether there had been any more bruises. Both John and Jenny were terrified that Laura would hurt herself again. She was more mobile now and getting into everything. No matter how closely they watched her, she still got into mischief. Books were dragged from bookshelves and ornaments were pulled off coffee tables. Miraculously, although she took a few knocks, she never had any visible bruises.

The summer arrived and the weather was glorious. The sun shone almost without interruption from June to September. John and Jenny spent as much time as possible in the cottage in Ashford and John managed to stay away from work for almost the entire month of August. Imelda Hennessy had told them that she, too, would be on leave throughout August and the tensions associated with her visits were temporarily forgotten. Every day Laura splashed around in the small green inflatable pool they had bought in a shop in Rathnew and she would gurgle with delight as she played with her yellow rubber duck or her blue plastic boat. After lunch she would fall asleep in her pram, shaded from the sun by the tall fir trees growing along the edge of the garden. Rebel would lie down nearby, keeping watch. The instant Laura woke, before she had a chance to cry out, he would quickly and quietly run to John or Jenny and pull at a skirt or trouser leg to let them know that she was awake and that it was time for a walk.

Occasionally, their peaceful solitude was interrupted by a visit from friends or relations, who continued to shower Laura with presents until everyone acknowledged that if any more baby clothes arrived, a new room would have to be built to accommodate them. Practically every toy that was kept in their Dublin home was duplicated in Ashford and John spent part of the first week in August making a toy cupboard in which to store the Wicklow toys.

Ruth and David and their children came to stay for the last week in August and John and Jenny made a great fuss of Susan and Declan, realising that since Laura's arrival they had seen far less of them. They were anxious to ensure that neither child should feel unloved or rejected by them.

They planned a seaside expedition. They crammed sandwiches, crisps, apples, bananas, cakes, baby food and Laura's bottle into a picnic hamper and twenty minutes after leaving Ashford they were all camped comfortably behind a sand dune at Brittas Bay. Susan and Declan happily built sand-castles, which Laura just as happily demolished with one blow of a small plastic spade. She was bounced in and out of the sea by John and giggled excitedly every time a wave broke around her. Rebel bounded in and out of the waves chasing an old tennis ball that Susan threw, barking enthusiastically every time it was pitched further into the water. As the day drew to a close, they drove slowly back to Ashford, stuck in a long line of Dublin-bound cars. Laura fell into a contented sleep in her car seat in the back of the car.

When the summer came to an end and autumn approached, John was back at work and Jenny and Laura fell back into their Dublin routine. In the middle of October Imelda Hennessy visited their home again and they found her just as difficult and unpleasant as she had been on all her previous visits. There was nothing new to tell her and she had nothing new to ask them. It was simply her unfriendly probing attitude that made them feel so uncomfortable. When they asked her how much longer it would take before she finished her report and everything would be completed by the Adoption Authority, she gave a non-committal reply.

* * *

By the time Laura had been with them for ten months her hair, still blonde, had grown into a thick mop. She could walk by holding on to the furniture or the wall but without support she would fall after two or three steps. She had discovered that if she threw a small ball Rebel would return it to her and they played this game together every day. At meal-times Rebel would still sit in the corner of the room, his sad brown eyes watching her adoringly. Laura's first words were Mama and Dada and Dog. Rebel had become "Dog" to all of them and without showing any resentment for this loss of identity, obediently answered to her call.

As his daughter grew, John acknowledged with amazement her similarity to Jenny. "She looks so much like her mother," was a comment made on countless occasions by acquaintances and others who did not know that Laura was being adopted. "The eyes are the giveaway," they would confidently explain and Jenny's eyes would sparkle with mischievous delight as she ran her fingers through her own long blonde hair.

One morning Mrs Gavin phoned and asked Jenny if it would be convenient if she called over to see them that evening. As they washed up after dinner, Jenny felt uneasy. Something in Mrs Gavin's voice worried her but she could not explain why she felt this way. She attributed her feelings to the nervousness felt by all adopters as the day of the hearing before the Adoption Authority approached. John, oblivious to her anxiety, whistled happily as he wiped the kitchen counter-top clean.

When they were all sitting in the lounge together, Jenny immediately noticed that Mrs Gavin had resumed the formal style of conversation she had used when they first met. A few minutes passed in polite chat before she came to her point.

"We have a difficulty," she said, without explaining who the "we" referred to. "Laura's mother has refused to sign the final consent and has asked that Laura be returned to her."

John and Jenny stared at her, dumbstruck, struggling to understand what they were being told.

"I'm sorry I have to bring this news to you," Mrs Gavin continued, "but this morning the society received a solicitor's letter threatening court proceedings. Until today we had hoped we could solve this problem without causing you worry."

She explained that for the previous two months Laura's biological mother had been confused as to what she wanted to do about her; that she had on three previous occasions asked for Laura to be returned to her but had each time changed her mind. This time, without forewarning, the society had received a letter from the mother's solicitor. They would have to reply to it.

"I have to ask you what you wish to do, whether you are agreeable to returning Laura to her biological mother?"

"No, we will not return her. We cannot," John replied quietly, surprised at his outward composure as his stomach knotted and his heart thumped.

"Why . . . why has she changed her mind now?" asked Jenny, feeling her control slipping away as the full implication of what Mrs Gavin had said exploded inside her. Before Mrs Gavin could reply she was shaken by sobs. She buried her head on John's shoulder and her body shook as her tears soaked through his shirt.

John turned helplessly to Mrs Gavin.

"What can we do? She is *our* child. She knows no other parents; she knows no other home. We love her so much." His voice trailed off as he felt a tear run down his cheek.

"You must see a lawyer, a solicitor, get legal advice," replied Mrs Gavin, the formality gone, her voice conveying sympathy and concern.

She had expected them to say no. Perhaps naïvely she had not anticipated that the intensity of their grief would penetrate her professional objectivity. Anger and tears she could understand, and resentment of her, of the society and of the mother for asking for Laura back. But this emotional appeal for help was different. Mrs Gavin had always been able to cope with tears, but the intensity of Jenny's reaction and the quiet pain in John's voice disarmed and deeply troubled her. She wanted to reach out and reassure them both that everything would be alright, that the mother would change her mind and co-operate again and that Laura could not be taken from them. But she could not do so because she could not mislead them in this way.

If they refused to return Laura she believed that it was unlikely that the mother would change her mind. A court case was therefore inevitable and she could not predict the result. She knew that the pain the Mastersons felt now could be replaced by far greater grief and anguish and that they would have to learn how to cope.

four

A slight blonde girl drove her Ford Fiesta up to the Kildare Street entrance of Leinster House and was waved through the gates by the Garda on duty. The Garda, a fresh young recruit from Roscommon, knew the girl's name and liked her pleasant and unassuming manner. He had previously tried to engage her in conversation when she was leaving the Dáil late in the evening. Her response had been friendly and they had had an animated chat about that night's unexpected political drama. Today, his observant eye noted that she was pale and that she returned his salute somewhat automatically.

For sixteen months, Colette James had been Dáil secretary to Seán Brannigan TD, a member of the Irish Parliament. It was her first job after leaving secretarial college. To ensure that she did not join the growing ranks of the unemployed in a country badly hit by recession, her parents had used their political connections to get her the position. Brannigan was their local TD and her father had originally helped him to secure a nomination as a Dáil candidate fifteen years earlier. At successive elections her father had campaigned for him and she frequently went along on the election trail, canvassing votes for Brannigan. He employed her by way of repayment for the political work both she and her father had undertaken voluntarily over the years.

Colette's first weeks working for Brannigan were uneventful. The glamour and status her parents believed attached to the job of a TD's secretary seemed remote from the daily drudgery of taking phone messages, arranging meetings with constituents, Dictaphone typing, responding to emails, keeping Brannigan's website up to date, photocopying and filing. The tedium was relieved by the occasional crank telephone call in response to a Brannigan speech and also by the Leinster House rumour factory. There was some political drama or scandal discussed over lunch practically every day. Sometimes these were true, mostly they were manufactured. Colette quickly discovered that the rumour machine attributed sexual adventures to Brannigan that contrasted sharply with his public utterances, but in her work for him she did not hear or see anything to substantiate the lunchtime talk.

Although he was forty-six years of age and married with three children, Brannigan looked younger than his years. Tall, with brown hair and blue eyes, he was a handsome man whose athletic appearance was more like that of a footballer than a politician. He was something of a political loner and seemed to spend more time in the company of the female parliamentary staff of Leinster House than with his political colleagues. Colette assumed that his friendliness towards the secretarial staff was the cause of much of the gossip about him.

Brannigan was only thirty-one years old when he was first elected to the Dáil to represent the Dublin West-Central constituency. An outspoken opponent of "artificial methods of contraception" and of divorce, he achieved national notoriety when, shortly after being elected, he had led from the back benches the parliamentary opposition to a constitutional change proposed to liberalised Ireland's restrictive divorce laws. From then on, he had frequently spoken out on what he described as "moral issues". He had been a successful Dáil candidate in six consecutive general elections, although ministerial rank had eluded him.

By the time Colette had started working as his parliamentary secretary, Seán Brannigan's public utterances had ceased to be confined to the "evils" of artificial contraception and the immorality of divorce. He had for some years adopted a far wider brief and had been presenting himself as a member of the emerging moral majority that would protect Ireland from socialists, communists and international conspiracies to subvert Christian morality – a conspiracy that was allegedly spearheaded by family planning clinics, abortion agencies and groups advocating gay marriage.

At public meetings, Brannigan boasted that his principal motivation in entering public life was "to preserve the sanctity of marriage and the family and to protect Ireland and its people from the sinful influences of the outside world". He publicly bemoaned the fact that book censorship was no longer protecting the youth of Ireland from the evil influences of foreign literature and perverse Irish writers. It pained him that the works of such writers were all now freely available. He regularly attacked the falling standards of Irish theatre and the frequent displays of nudity on stage and lamented the failure of the film censor to ban sexually explicit films.

Brannigan also projected himself as a law and order politician. He was publicly contemptuous of "flabby liberal" politicians and he wanted to restore capital punishment. Murderers should be hanged, crooks and thugs should be jailed and if the Gardaí broke a few limbs or knocked out a few teeth when making arrests, Seán Brannigan would not lose any sleep over it.

As a supporter of the pro-life movement, Brannigan was a leading proponent for a constitutional amendment and legislation to prevent Irish women having abortions abroad in order to protect the Irish unborn against the "abortionists in England and the rest of the world". He argued that a constitutional prohibition on abortion in Ireland had no value unless measures were taken to prevent pregnant Irish women terminating their pregnancies elsewhere.

Every journalist in Ireland knew that on a dull news day Seán Brannigan could be relied upon for a quotable and controversial comment. He was both pro-life and pro-hanging and neither he nor his supporters saw any contradiction in his stance on these issues or in his public utterances.

Colette had known Brannigan since her childhood when they had developed a relationship like that of uncle and niece. She assumed when she first came to work for him that they would have a more formal relationship than they had had in the past. Brannigan, however, insisted that they be on first-name terms.

Colette found him to be a very conscientious deputy. He invariably worked from early morning until well after midnight, devoting half of his working day to humdrum constituency duties and the remaining portion of his time to researching, composing and delivering speeches in the Dáil chamber or at party or public meetings – speeches that were nearly always controversial and, occasionally, outrageous.

For a few months after Colette had started at Leinster House, she frequently worked late into the night and, on these occasions, she and Seán Brannigan would usually eat an evening meal together. At first he discussed only politics with her. Five months after she began to work for him, he started to speak of his family and personal life. He complained that his wife enjoyed the status conferred by his position but deeply resented the hours he worked. According to him, his wife had been very young when they had married and they had grown apart over the years and were no longer sleeping together. They had remained living in the one house to preserve the public perception that they had a happy marriage and more particularly in order to maintain his public image.

Colette was astonished at Brannigan's revelation of his marital problems. Her sympathy for him grew as he revealed more to her about his unhappy marriage. Their relationship rapidly deepened. She ceased to be a foster-niece or a mere Dáil secretary and became his intimate confidante. Their meals together were no longer confined to the dull impersonal surroundings of the Dáil restaurant. Seán Brannigan entered into a regular pairing arrangement with a friendly TD from another party so that they both could miss Dáil votes without affecting the voting strength of their own parties, and he and Colette regularly ventured outside the precincts of Leinster House to try out the food in one of Dublin's many small and intimate restaurants. On those occasions when they could not eat together because of Brannigan's political commitments, Colette missed his company.

After she had worked for a year in Leinster House, Colette James felt that she knew more about Seán Brannigan than about any other person she had ever known. One evening as she sat in the lounge of her parents' house, paying no heed to the story of adventure and intrigue that so engrossed her mother and father from the blaring television set, she realised that her restless thoughts were dominated by the immaculately dressed, handsome legislator for whom she worked. Colette struggled to dismiss him from her mind but battled with herself in vain. She recalled a similar experience when as a young impressionable teenager she had canvassed with Brannigan and her father in an election campaign and had become infatuated with the tall good-humoured TD with whom her father was so friendly. In those days he used to sweep her up in his arms, plant a playful kiss on her nose and talk of her as his "little cherub". He had not done that since she had turned fifteen and she now fearfully realised that she again wanted to run to him and to be swept off her feet. Colette was gripped by a strange sensation and shuddered. Unwittingly she had become repossessed by a teenage sexual fantasy and it was now too late for her to turn back. Like intrepid explorers before her, she was about to discover how the mirages of the teenage mind can on occasion predict the realities of a future life.

* * *

Seán Brannigan had travelled the same road before, but never with a secretary he had known since she was a small child. He told himself that it was not his fault that the young secretaries around Leinster House were attracted to him. But somehow Colette was different because he was able to relate to her in a way that had never proved possible with the others. For the first few months she worked for him he had deliberately held back, fearful of what could happen if he pressurised her in some way and she went to her father. Instead, he had allowed their relationship to evolve and mature slowly and now, as they lay silently beside each other, he knew that he had been right.

Her inexperienced hands touched him so tentatively that every muscle in his body ached for fulfilment. When he entered her, he knew it was her first time. He moved slowly and she dug her fingers into his back, moaning and gasping for breath. When she loosened her grip and her body relaxed, he knew he was going to erupt. She gasped again as he pulled himself free of her and overflowed on her slender body. They were lying on the carpeted floor of his office, the office in which Colette had been working for thirteen months. No sounds came from the empty rooms above and below them. It was almost midnight and, except for the Gardaí at the entrance gates, Leinster House was deserted. No one was there to witness Seán Brannigan and Colette James becoming lovers.

* * *

Colette parked, turned off the ignition, stepped out of her car and walked uncertainly towards the imposing entrance to Leinster House. Her mind was numb with shock. She felt her legs go weak and held desperately onto the spinning doors. She did not know how he would react or what he would do. Two months earlier he told her he was going to apply to the Roman Catholic Church for a decree annulling his marriage, so that they could marry in church, but she knew that he had done nothing to start the process. He was still living with his wife and she knew nothing of their relationship.

It had never occurred to Colette that this could happen. She knew that she had been foolish for not taking the necessary precautions herself, but Brannigan had assured her that he always withdrew in time and that she was not at risk. She now knew this to be untrue. Her condition had been confirmed. Colette James, convent-educated, twenty years of age and unmarried, was going to be a mother. Seán Brannigan TD had fathered his fourth child. It would be born in seven months' time.

* * *

Colette could not sleep that night. She lay awake, recalling the day's events: the cheerful doctor who had confirmed her pregnancy earlier that morning, unaware of her single status and unspoken anguish; the support and comfort offered by Sally Thomas, the secretary of David Brewer TD, whose office was next to hers; the horror registering on Seán Brannigan's face upon her breaking the news to him; the speed with which the intimacy between them had disintegrated.

Brannigan's shocked reaction had quickly turned to anger and accusation.

"It's your own fault!" he shouted as he strode across to the window, then turned to face her again. "How stupid not to take precautions! You should have been on the pill!"

He silenced her protests with an impatient wave of his hand. He paced the floor, pausing only to throw a question or an accusation at her, never waiting for her answer, never listening at all.

"What other men have you been with? How do I know I'm the father? How many others were there?"

"There are no others," she replied, sobbing uncontrollably, the tears running down her cheeks onto her dress. "There is nobody, only you."

He offered her no help, no sympathy.

"We will both be ruined if this gets out!" He was shouting and ignoring her distress. As the full impact of her news dawned on him, his eyes took on a haunted look. The anger subsided and was replaced by fear and despair. He stopped shouting and sat down, staring at her.

Rocking backwards and forwards in his chair as if in a trance, he asked in a whisper, "What are you going to do?"

"I don't know. What can I do?" she replied, her voice trembling, grateful that at last he was showing some concern for her. But his next question cruelly shattered the illusion.

"Have you considered an abortion?" His voice was hesitant and he would not meet her eyes.

The words echoed in her head as she lay awake in bed. Brannigan's concern had been for himself, *not* for her. Her condition terrified him and his reaction had appalled her. She had not replied to his question but had rushed into the toilet, faint and nauseous. Before she returned to his office, Brannigan had fled.

How could he of all people suggest an abortion? She would not have an abortion. She could not. She would have her baby. But what then? Should she keep it or would she have it adopted? Would it be a boy or a girl? How would her parents react? How would she look after it? Would they help her?

Her head swimming with questions she could not answer, Colette fell into a deep but troubled sleep. In the dark of the night, above the sound of the rain beating against the bedroom window, something or someone whispered to her that it was just a nightmare, that she would be alright in the morning, that she had imagined it all. But sitting down for breakfast the next morning she felt sick and could not eat. She knew it was not her imagination, that she was not dreaming, that it was real.

Colette was pregnant and unmarried. She was living her own private nightmare and she had to cope.

five

Colette could not tell her parents the truth. She told them she wanted to be independent and that she did not want to live at home until the day she married. She moved into a flat with Sally Thomas, in whom she had already confided the news about her pregnancy.

For the next few months she continued to work as Seán Brannigan's secretary. She had no alternative because she needed the income. They had a formal business-like relationship now. Colette told him that she would not have an abortion and that she would finally decide what to do after the baby was born. He did not again speak of a church annulment or of their marrying. Instead he pleaded with Colette not to tell his wife and she assured him that she had told no one other than Sally Thomas. He offered her money but she would take none.

The weeks passed uneventfully. Colette's conversations with Brannigan were stilted and difficult but they maintained an outwardly cordial working relationship, each meticulously avoiding any references to her condition. She arranged for the baby to be born in the Rotunda Hospital, went for monthly medical check-ups and spent most evenings in the flat watching television. She visited her parents each weekend but they remained ignorant of her pregnancy.

It only started to show in the sixth month and she concealed it well behind loose, sack-like dresses. At work she talked of going on a diet and she believed the other secretaries thought she was overweight. She did not know that she had been the main topic of the rumour machine for months. Seven weeks before the baby was due, she went on sick leave. A few days later she made an appointment to visit St Mark's Adoption Society.

* * *

Immediately on her arrival at St Mark's, Colette was ushered in to see a social worker. Betty Comerford reached for Colette's hand and shook it firmly, inviting her to sit down at a small coffee table positioned beside a window in the corner of her office overlooking the street.

Colette examined her nervously. She was about five feet tall, looked to be in her mid-forties, wore a dark brown and beige tartan jacket and skirt, and had long black hair tied up in a bun. Her hair gave her a severe look, which often misled those who first met her into believing that she lacked any real sympathy for their plight. Because she had already made the decision to have her baby adopted, Colette was anxious to get to the point of her visit and make whatever arrangements were necessary.

Mrs Comerford listened to her attentively.

Without interruption Colette told her story and concluded: "I don't want anyone to know the name of the father. I want the baby to go to adopters immediately after its birth."

Mrs Comerford was sympathetic but cautious. She urged Colette not to make a final decision until after the baby was born and said that Colette could contact her at any time and that she would do whatever she could to be of help. She was particularly concerned about Colette's desire to conceal her pregnancy from her parents.

"Would you not consider telling them?" she asked. "Although some parents react with hostility, many are sympathetic and helpful."

"I can't tell them. It would kill my mother. She would not understand," Colette responded, firmly and quietly.

In reply to Mrs Comerford's questions about the father of her baby, she just said he knew she was pregnant and that there was no possibility of marriage. She was adamant – her baby was to be adopted. Adoption would be best for the baby and for her. She would not change her mind.

Mrs Comerford explained the adoption process

to Colette and outlined the various steps involved. Colette insisted that she wished the baby to be adopted straight from hospital since she could not bring it home or care for it. She wanted it to have a good home from the start and did not want it placed in an institution.

"Is it possible for me to sign the papers for the adoption here and now?"

"You can't do that just yet. You have to wait until the baby is born. If you phone me then, I will visit you in hospital and we'll be able to make all the necessary arrangements."

As Colette drove away from St Mark's the pressures of the previous weeks seemed to lift from her shoulders. She had made her decision and she knew it was for the best. The baby would be born and adopted and she could then resume her normal life as if she had never been pregnant.

When Sally Thomas returned home that evening, she was surprised to find Colette singing in the kitchen, busily cooking a curry for them both. The sombre and depressing atmosphere that had hung over the flat seemed to have lifted. They drank a little wine that night and gossiped. Sally was relieved that Colette had come to terms with her situation and had made a firm decision.

Colette awoke at three o'clock the next morning. Her head was throbbing and she realised she had a slight hangover. She lay in bed semi-conscious. The baby suddenly kicked out and it felt like it was trying to kick its way out of her body. It was almost as if the small being inside her knew it was going to be given away, knew that she was rejecting it and was now making clear its rejection of her. A nagging doubt entered Colette's mind. Was she making the right decision? She could not stop thinking how terrible it must be for a baby never to be touched or cuddled by its own mother, never to know its own father or to be loved by its real grandparents. She started to sob quietly to herself. Though she still believed her decision was right, she was no longer certain. Her head lay still on the soft wet pillow as she cried herself to sleep.

six

Colette gripped the nurse's hand tightly and pushed. Beads of perspiration dripped from her forehead onto her nose. She felt a strange pressure in the lower part of her body, but no pain. The epidural was doing its job.

The nurse gently stroked her forehead with a cold flannel and smiled.

"You're doing fine. It won't be long now," she said.

The monitor registered another contraction.

"Push, push again," the nurse said and Colette obeyed her orders. The contractions were now coming very rapidly.

Colette asked the nurse her name.

"Laura," she replied.

"How long have you been in maternity?"

"For over five years. Now get ready. Here comes another contraction."

Colette pushed and as she did so the gynaecologist walked into the room.

"How soon, nurse?" he asked as his hands gently felt the top of Colette's swollen stomach.

"Very soon now."

"You're doing fine, Colette," he said, acknowledging her presence. "Now just relax."

The monitor registered another contraction and she pushed again, this time without being told.

"That's right, that's fine," she heard the nurse say in her soothing voice. "Any minute now you'll see your baby's head if you look in the mirror behind the doctor."

Another contraction and a push.

"Here it comes," the doctor announced. Propping herself up on her elbows, Colette saw the reflection of her baby's head in the mirror.

"That's it, keep on pushing," a voice said. "It's coming, it's almost there! . . . It's a girl!"

Colette heard a scissors cutting and saw her baby daughter in the nurse's arms. She heard a high-pitched cry. Without warning, the nurse laid the baby on her stomach and the crying stopped. The baby was small and wizened-looking, like an ancient leprechaun. Colette thought she was beautiful. She lay there looking into her baby's face as the doctor worked in the background and another nurse said something about getting her tidied up. The nurse whose name was Laura gently lifted the baby away.

"She's seven pounds seven ounces," said the nurse

as she weighed the baby on a small scales and then gently wiped her down.

Colette was in a daze. The lower part of her body still felt numb and her head was swimming. She imagined she was floating above the room watching someone else giving birth, as if she was a spectator, not a participant. She had entered a timeless twilight zone and was merely a cloud floating through it. In her mind she could still see the reflection of the baby's head in the mirror at the other end of the room and again she heard a high-pitched cry. Then she realised that the noise was coming from beside her. Looking down she saw a small head with its body neatly wrapped in a pink sheet lying next to her.

Half an hour later Colette lay propped up in bed drinking a cup of tea, her daughter asleep in a little glass cot beside her bed.

"What are you going to call her?" the nurse asked.

"I am not going to give her a name," Colette replied. "I'm having her adopted."

"Oh, I see, I didn't realise," the nurse stuttered in reply, surprise registering on her face.

"I'm not married," Colette explained simply.

"I see, I'm sorry," said the nurse.

"Don't be sorry. You've been very good to me. I'm grateful. I felt so alone when I arrived. You were very kind."

Before going to sleep that night Colette instructed the sister in charge of the ward that she did not want to see her baby again. The glass cot was not to be wheeled in to her the next morning.

* * *

Shortly after Colette had finished her breakfast the hospital registrar called to her room. A tall grey-haired woman in her early sixties and dressed in black, she looked more like a headmistress. She needed particulars in order to register the baby's birth and wanted to know what name Colette had chosen. Colette explained about the adoption and the registrar promised to contact Mrs Comerford in St Mark's for her.

"Even if she is to be adopted, her birth has to be registered," the registrar explained. "I can register her simply as Baby James if you wish, but most mothers in your position give their child a name."

Colette had maintained her composure since the delivery but now she felt it starting to slip. She had twice explained to nurses why she would not breastfeed and had resisted their suggestions that she should do so at least for the few days that she would remain in hospital. She had explained to the Sister why she did not wish to see her daughter again and had withstood her curt reply. The amiability of the gynaecologist had seemed artificial to her when he examined her that morning and she thought she had detected a tone of disapproval. Colette now found it impossible to ignore the contempt she felt she saw in this woman's eyes because she was refusing even to name her child.

As the registrar got up to leave, Colette called out. "Wait a minute, wait, I think I will give her a name."

The registrar sat down again slowly.

"What do you want to call her?" she asked.

"I'll call her Laura," Colette replied quietly, thinking of the kind and gentle nurse whose hand she had gripped so tightly in the delivery room the previous day.

* * *

Colette remained in hospital for five days. On the third day she was visited by Mrs Comerford. This was only their second meeting, but her friendly and relaxed manner came as a relief to Colette. She behaved more like a sympathetic grandmother than a social worker.

"How are you?" she asked, genuine concern reflected in her face.

"I'm fine, I think," Colette replied, pleased that she had come. "The soreness seems to be going. I was lucky I didn't need any stitches. The poor woman in the room next door had to have eight stitches and spends most of the day sitting in baths filled with salt."

They both laughed.

"You picked a good week," Mrs Comerford said.

"It hasn't stopped raining for the past three days. I wouldn't mind a few days in bed myself at the moment."

"I'm glad you came," Colette said. "I have not changed my mind. I still want Laura, my baby, to be adopted." She had not meant to use the name she had so unwillingly given to her baby.

"I see," said Mrs Comerford. "There's no hurry, no rush. You can think it over a bit longer if you want to."

"No, I'm certain," Colette replied. "I've refused to see her since she was born. I can't take her home. I can't look after her and I don't want to make it any more difficult for her or for me."

"You called her Laura?" Mrs Comerford asked.

"After the nurse in the delivery room," Colette explained, but volunteered no more information.

"I can arrange for Laura to go from here to temporary foster parents after you leave if you want a little more time," Mrs Comerford suggested.

"No, that would be unfair to her," Colette replied firmly. "I want her placed with a family for adoption as soon as possible. I don't want her to go to foster parents. I've made my decision and I won't change my mind."

"Do your parents know that you've had a baby?" Mrs Comerford asked.

"No," Colette replied, her voice trembling with emotion. "They think I have gone abroad for a holiday. They never discovered I was pregnant and I never told them. I couldn't; they wouldn't understand. They would never talk to me again if they knew. The only person who knows I have been here, other than you, is my flatmate, Sally Thomas."

They were interrupted by a nurse bringing in a pot of tea and biscuits with one cup and a saucer. Colette asked for a second cup and Mrs Comerford accepted her offer of tea. The nurse, putting down the second cup, looked up at Colette.

"Are you sure you don't want to see your baby today?" she asked.

"Why do I have to explain to every nurse who comes on duty?" Colette exclaimed, exasperation and anger in her voice. "I don't want to see the baby. I don't ever want to see her again. I don't want the baby to see me. It's better that way. Why does everybody keep on asking me to see her?"

"I'm sorry . . . I didn't mean to upset you." The nurse's voice trailed off as she retreated from the room, taken aback by the ferocity of Colette's reaction.

"Well, if everyone didn't keep on asking me bloody silly questions, I wouldn't get upset!" Colette shouted after her.

Mrs Comerford picked up the pot of tea and poured some out for both of them.

"Do you take milk?" she asked, breaking the silence.

"Yes, yes please," Colette replied as a tear slowly ran down her cheek. "I'm sorry. It's not the nurses' fault – they mean well," she said as the cup of tea was handed to her.

"It's alright, I understand," Mrs Comerford responded. "I know it's not easy."

They discussed adoption. Mrs Comerford arranged to visit Colette on the morning she was leaving hospital. She could then complete the adoption forms authorising St Mark's to place Laura with a family for adoption. Later on she would have to sign another form and could change her mind at any time before an adoption order was made by the Adoption Authority. However, if she did change her mind, Laura would not automatically be returned to her. If the adopters refused to co-operate, it would be left to the courts to decide whether Laura should remain with the adopters or be returned to Colette.

Colette was anxious to sign whatever forms had to be signed and was adamant that she would not change her mind. She wished to forget the past nine months and to forget about Laura. She wanted everything finalised as quickly as possible.

Two days later, Mrs Comerford came to the hospital again. Witnessing Colette's signature on the adoption form, she explained to her that Laura would remain in the maternity hospital overnight and be collected by someone from St Mark's the following day in order to be placed with adoptive parents.

"I think you should at least see Laura again before you leave here," Mrs Comerford counselled Colette. "You may think it better not to do so now, but some time in the future you may regret not seeing her other than on the day she was born. Please consider what I am saying, Colette."

Colette knew that she could not see her baby again. In her own mind Laura was already something in her past. She had started to convince herself that she had been in hospital recovering from an illness. Colette was now going home and did not want to reawaken any memories; her main desire was to forget that she had ever been pregnant or had given birth. To her, Laura had ceased to exist.

"There is no point in my seeing her again. It would achieve nothing," she replied and Mrs Comerford did not press her further.

* * *

Three weeks later Colette went back to work. During her absence Seán Brannigan TD had acquired a new secretary, a grey-haired fifty-six-year-old widow, the sister of another TD. Just a week before Colette was to return, a new TD had been elected in a by-election in Tipperary East. He and Brannigan were members of the same party and Colette had been asked by phone whether she would work for him. She was told that Brannigan was anxious to retain his new secretary, who originally had been employed on a temporary basis until Colette "recovered from her illness". Colette was relieved that she did not have to resume her job as Brannigan's secretary and readily agreed. She settled down well and liked her new boss.

Michael O'Brien was tall, twenty-eight years of age, dark and single. Still surprised at his electoral success, he was overawed by his surroundings and his political colleagues.

"They were all just names in the papers and faces on television until last week," he explained to Colette on her first day back. He seemed relieved to have someone to talk to.

"They're only people, like you and me," Colette assured him. "No different, you will see."

She liked working for him. He was quiet, modest and undemanding. As the weeks passed, she helped him to settle into political life, organising his constituency appointments, teaching him how to deal with the intricacies of government departments and prickly ministers and running off circular letters to his constituents, thanking all those who voted for him and helped him during the election campaign.

Even as the weeks passed and Michael O'Brien settled in, he retained his shyness and did not develop that look of self-importance that, Colette felt, attached to even the most unimportant of the elected inhabitants of Leinster House.

Colette managed to block Laura out of her mind completely. She joined a musical society and twice a week participated in rehearsals for a small part she was to play in an amateur production of *The Mikado*. Two other evenings a week she played squash.

Colette still shared a flat with Sally Thomas and for the first time she really enjoyed the freedom of not living with her parents and of not always having to explain over the breakfast table where she had been the night before. She and Seán Brannigan rarely saw each other; if they did occasionally pass in the corridors of Leinster House, he would nod guiltily in her direction. Colette learned to avert her eyes when she saw him approaching and no look of recognition registered on her face; she just kept on walking.

One weekend when she was paying her regular visit to her parents, they told her she was looking well and that they were pleased she was enjoying her job. They had been concerned about her when she seemed to be getting very overweight but noticed that since her return from holidays she had regained her slim figure and vivacious looks. Her mother suspected that she had spent the three weeks away in one of those health spas, but did not say anything to her because she felt Colette was entitled to keep such things secret. Both her parents were pleased that she had become Michael O'Brien's secretary and hoped that one day their daughter might marry a TD. One night lying in bed they talked in whispers of the possibility of Colette being the wife of a future minister or taoiseach. They were both delighted that their suggestion that she should become a Dáil secretary over two years earlier had worked out so well.

seven

Three months after his election, Colette accompanied Michael O'Brien to the theatre. It was during the Dublin Theatre Festival and, as a TD, he had received two complimentary tickets to a new production of a Tom Murphy play. Until then Colette and he had never met outside Leinster House and had enjoyed a strictly working relationship. She had arranged to play squash that evening and initially refused his invitation.

"I'm sorry. I shouldn't have embarrassed you by asking you to go out with me," he said meekly, disappointment registering on his face as his cheeks turned red.

Colette saw that he was uncomfortable and felt guilty. She had not gone out on a date with anyone since she had resumed work and was afraid of having anything other than a formal working relationship with the young TD. Yet he was different from Brannigan.

Michael O'Brien was nearer to her age. He was single and obviously lonely and still somewhat lost and unsure of himself in the strange political environment of Leinster House. She decided to accept the invitation.

It was an enjoyable evening; the play was funny and they both laughed a lot. They continued laughing as they ate hamburgers and chips in Captain America's Cookhouse in Grafton Street after the show. He talked of his canvassing experience during the by-election and told her about some of the comical incidents that had taken place. She filled him in on some of the political gossip of the previous two years. Two hours later he dropped her home to her flat and drove off with a simple goodnight after thanking her for going out with him.

During the following months the friendship between Colette and Michael O'Brien grew. They ate together in the Leinster House restaurant more frequently and she again went out with him to the theatre.

One evening Colette accompanied him to a ministerial function. On the way they stopped off at the home of his sister, Jane, and brother-in-law, Brian, to give them an anniversary present. As they all sat talking around the kitchen table, Colette was suddenly taken aback by the sound of a baby crying.

"That's Kevin," Jane explained, going out of the room. "He's due his feed."

A few minutes later she reappeared, carrying a plumpish, red-cheeked baby in a blue Babygro.

Colette suddenly broke out in a cold sweat and started to shiver. She wanted to ask the baby's age but couldn't utter a sound. All she could do was silently watch Jane as she sat back in her chair, unselfconsciously unbuttoned the front of her blouse and slipped her right nipple into the baby's mouth. The room that had seemed so warm and pleasant to Colette a few minutes earlier now felt cold and threatening.

"How old is he?" she managed to ask, relieved that her lips were again responding to her thoughts but disturbed by the strange croaking sound of her voice.

"Four months," came the reply.

Colette couldn't think of anything else to say and was glad that all eyes were concentrated on the baby and that no notice was being taken of her. A strange sensation came over her and she thought she was going to collapse. She had last felt like this when she was telling Brannigan of her pregnancy. Now she knew she was going to get sick.

"The toilet, where is the toilet?" she managed to ask Jane.

"First door on the right down the hall," came the reply.

She stood up slowly, not wishing to draw too much attention to herself and walked unsteadily out of the kitchen. Her steps quickened as she walked down the hall, and she reached the bathroom just in time.

Ten minutes later she returned to the kitchen.

"Are you alright?" Michael asked, concerned. "You look very white."

"I feel a little peculiar," she admitted. "It must be something I ate. I don't think I'm going to be able to make it to the function."

Michael drove her home. Colette resisted his offer to take her to a doctor.

"It's only an upset stomach and I'll take something for it myself."

As she got out of the car she apologised for spoiling his night and for not talking much in the car and said she would see him the next day. Entering the hall, she saw her reflection in the mirror and was shocked. Her face had a corpse-like appearance. She looked as if she had aged ten years.

Still feeling cold and shivery, Colette quickly slipped into her nightdress and climbed into bed. She lay in bed, intimidated by the quietness of the flat and the darkness of the room. Finding that she could not sleep, she reached out and turned on the bedside light and attempted to read. Ten minutes later she realised that she was just turning pages, ignorant of the contents of what she had read, her mind unable to concentrate. She put down the book, switched on the radio and laid her head on the pillow as the sound of Michael Bublé filled the room. Lying there, staring into nothingness, Colette fought to overcome the despair that was engulfing her. Suddenly she was falling into a bottomless pit and, as she fell, she could see reflected on the walls of the pit disjointed images of two hideously shaped legs between which protruded the top of a baby's head. She felt a searing pain in her groin and cried out. Somewhere in the distance a voice kept saying, "It's a girl . . . It's a girl . . . It's a girl."

The voice grew louder and louder as she continued to fall. She started to scream, the tears pouring down her cheeks as she shook from side to side.

"Come on, Colette, wake up, you're dreaming. You're having a nightmare, you're going to be alright," a voice said.

She stopped falling and became conscious of music. Someone was stroking her head. She opened her eyes and blinked at the brightness of the bedside lamp.

"You had a nightmare," Sally repeated soothingly, as she gently stroked Colette's cheek. "You'll be alright now."

eight

The nightmare came back the following night and the night after that and kept on recurring. Colette found she was unable to eat or sleep properly. Every time she drove or walked past a child, she thought of Laura. She wondered what her daughter looked like, what she was eating, what clothes she was wearing, how tall she was, whether she was crawling. Colette's head was filled with questions she could not answer.

She relived the birth scene over and over again. Not just in her nightmares but now during the day. Especially the moment when the newborn Laura had been placed on top of her. She yearned to feel again the warmth of Laura's soft skin next to her own body. More than anything else, she wanted to reach out and touch her, to trace her fingers over her face, stroke her body and to hold her close and cuddle her.

Colette started to feel ashamed that she had abandoned Laura to strangers and guilty for not having tried to care for her herself. She kept on telling herself that she had made the right decision. Sally repeatedly expressed the same view but Colette no longer believed it to be true.

She had not seen Mrs Comerford, her social worker, since she had signed the adoption papers. Now she decided to contact her, although not at all sure what she was going to say or what she was going to do. She told Sally Thomas that she might take Laura back and get a flat of her own but Sally insisted that she remain living with her. If Colette decided to bring Laura up herself, she would need some help, at least in the beginning, and Sally would not hear of her moving out.

Twice Colette phoned St Mark's to make an appointment to see Mrs Comerford. On both occasions she just wanted to ask for an appointment but each time she found herself blurting out that she wanted Laura back and then put down the phone before Mrs Comerford could respond or arrange a meeting with her. Both times she phoned back later the same day to say that she had changed her mind again and still believed that Laura should be adopted.

Colette's thoughts were in turmoil and she did not know what to do or who to turn to. She stayed away from work and stopped going out at night. She would not answer the phone and refused to return calls from Michael O'Brien. Her weekend visits home to her parents stopped on the pretext of her involvement in a forthcoming musical. Constantly she talked of Laura to

Sally but despite Sally's encouragement she refused to contact Mrs Comerford again or to discuss her problem with her parents.

One evening Michael O'Brien called to see Colette but he did not get past Sally who, on Colette's orders, told him that she was sleeping. After three weeks had passed without Colette stepping outside the flat, Sally decided she would take the initiative. She went to see Colette's parents.

* * *

The ferocity of Mr and Mrs James' reaction was something that Sally had not anticipated. She had expected they would be surprised and upset but the anger and hostility which her visit to them provoked startled her. They did not believe her at first and accused her of lying. When they accepted that she was speaking the truth their disbelief turned to panic. They cursed Colette's stupidity, and at the same time expressed hurt that they had only now been told and relief that the child had been placed for adoption.

"We don't want to see Colette. And we don't want to see the baby. We couldn't tolerate her coming back to our house with a baby," Bill James angrily insisted, despite Sally's plea that they visit Colette.

They had provided Colette with the best of everything – a good education, a good home, a good job. How could she do this to them? What would their neighbours and friends say if they knew?

Sally left their house feeling dazed. Though she had read of such reactions in books and had seen similar behaviour played out in films and plays, to her this type of response had always seemed unreal, almost a caricature. She had not believed Colette when she spoke of how her parents would react if they knew the truth and thought her friend was exaggerating, but now she knew Colette had been right. Sally realised that she was going to have to tell Colette of her visit and knew her intervention had been disastrous. She had exacerbated an already serious situation. Fortunately, she had not revealed the father's identity.

* * *

Colette looked devastated when Sally told her the story of her visit.

"Why didn't you tell me first?" she asked. "I always knew how they would react."

"I'm so sorry," Sally replied. "I thought I was doing the right thing. I thought it was for the best and that they would offer you help if you took Laura back. I was wrong and you were right all the time. I'm really sorry."

"But what am I to do now?" Colette asked helplessly, too overcome by events to be angry with Sally. "Should I contact them – phone them or go to see them? What should I do?"

"I don't know," answered Sally, afraid to make another wrong decision.

"Perhaps I should visit them," Colette continued. "I should at least try to explain now that they know."

"Perhaps," replied Sally. "I don't know what advice to give you."

"I can't just ignore the fact that they know. Maybe I should just put my coat on and drive over there now."

"Don't you think you should give them time to come to terms with it?" Sally asked hesitatingly. "Perhaps leave it until tomorrow?"

"No, I think I should go now," Colette replied.

* * *

As she got out of the car outside the house she had lived in for twenty years of her life, Colette felt for the first time like a stranger in her own neighbourhood. Although she still had a key to the door, she rang the bell. Her mother opened the door and they stood there staring at each other. Colette could see she had been crying. Her father came out into the hall. The look on his face terrified her. It was not her father she saw approaching but a strange and angry man shaking his fist violently in the air.

"Is it true?" he roared. "Do you have a baby?"

"Yes, it's true," she replied, her voice quivering.

"You're no daughter of mine!" he shouted. "I don't know you. Your mother doesn't know you. We don't want to know you. Don't set foot in this house again."

His face had now turned red with emotion. Colette

thought he might hit her. She backed away and then turned and ran down the garden path to her car, the tears streaming down her cheeks, the sound of her mother's hysterical sobbing following her. With difficulty she opened the car door and drove blindly away, just avoiding hitting a pedestrian who was crossing the road in front of her.

* * *

Two days later the letter arrived from St Mark's. Mrs Comerford wanted Colette to arrange an appointment to sign the final adoption papers. She also expressed concern about the phone calls Colette had made to her. Even if Colette was not yet ready to sign the papers, she was very anxious that Colette call in for a chat with her.

The arrival of the letter had a strangely calming effect on Colette. She realised that she was now going to have to make a final decision. Laura's future was still in her hands. She had not yet completely lost her. She phoned and made an appointment to see Betty Comerford.

* * *

It was raining as Colette parked her car outside the grey façade of St Mark's. Mrs Comerford had been very friendly on the phone and had repeated that she was most anxious to talk to her. As Colette locked the car door and walked up the steps to the door, she wondered how the adoption society would react to her request that Laura be returned to her. She had now made up her mind. She wanted Laura back.

Colette sank into the brown-leather armchair opposite Mrs Comerford's desk.

"How are you, Colette?" the older woman asked.

Colette felt edgy. She had rehearsed what she would say and wanted to get straight to it. Her tension was heightened by her belief that Mrs Comerford would react aggressively and she was not certain how she would respond in that case.

"I want Laura back," she blurted out. "I've made a terrible mistake. I can't give her up. I need her and I believe she needs me!"

Mrs Comerford's face showed no surprise. Her only reaction was to ask, "Are you sure?"

Colette's nervousness made her say more than she had meant to. What she had intended to be a brief meeting developed into an hour-long discussion of the reason for her decision, her ability to care for Laura, the attitude of her parents and the effects on Laura of such a dramatic change at this stage in her development.

Mrs Comerford was sympathetic. Many mothers suffer similar doubts. She should not feel guilty. Laura had settled in well with the adopters and was very much a part of their family. She urged Colette not to make a final decision but to think it over further.

"It would be unfair to the adopters to ask that they return Laura unless you are absolutely certain."

Taken aback by Mrs Comerford's reasonableness and her logical, unemotional reaction, Colette again felt a terrible sense of uncertainty.

"You do realise," Mrs Comerford continued, "that Laura will not know you? In her world the adopters are her mother and father and you are just a stranger. If she moves from the adopters' home and is cut off from them and everything that is familiar to her, she will experience a great feeling of loss for a time and will become very distressed. You will not only have to care for her but you will have to establish a relationship with her at a time of very great emotional upset in her young life. It will be far more difficult than the usual role played by a mother when she returns home from hospital with her new-born baby."

Colette's doubts grew. She felt that she wanted Laura back but now her head signalled something different. Realising that nothing was going to be settled at this meeting, she decided to bring it to an end.

"Give me some more time to think, please," she said, slowly rising from her chair.

"You have all the time you want," Mrs Comerford replied, holding her hand out to Colette. "I will give you whatever help I can in making a final decision, but before you make that decision you must fully understand all the possible consequences for Laura."

* * *

As she walked down the steps of St Mark's Colette felt dazed. An hour earlier she had walked up the same steps certain of her decision. Then the uncertainty had returned because of what Mrs Comerford had said to her. Once out of Mrs Comerford's presence and the claustrophobic atmosphere of her interview room, she realised that she still wanted Laura back. She could not understand why she had agreed again to postpone acting on her decision. Colette was emotionally drained. Mrs Comerford, she believed, had deliberately confused her. She was no longer a friend who could offer her help, but an obstacle, cutting her off from Laura.

That night as she lay in bed Colette tried to remember what Laura looked like and realised that she could no longer fully recall the features of the tiny wizened face that had lain beside her in the delivery room. In the silent bedroom she could hear her own heart pounding and a knot in her stomach seemed to pulse in time with the beat. As she drifted into a troubled sleep the knot developed into a tiny being beside her.

At around four o'clock in the morning she awoke with a start. She felt as if something had just kicked out in the pit of her stomach. Momentarily she thought she was still pregnant and that her baby was again protesting against being adopted. She now knew that not only did she want Laura back, but that Laura was also reaching out to her and wanted to come home. Her daughter wanted to be with her real mother and did not care whether she ever saw the adopters again. Colette knew that Betty Comerford was wrong. Laura wanted to return to her and she was convinced that when she did return everything would work out alright.

nine

It was almost four weeks since Colette had been at work in Leinster House. She had reported sick and the local doctor who knew of her "problem", as he described her situation, agreed to give her a medical certificate to cover the period she had been out of work. The certificate said she needed a further week to recuperate. She had come in now, not to work but to keep an appointment she had made with Michael O'Brien. In addition to trying to visit her in her flat, he had attempted to contact her by phone on half-a-dozen occasions while she was out "sick", but she had never been able to bring herself to talk to him. Sally had put him off and passed on messages from Colette about appointments and meetings she had arranged for him.

She stood in the lift as it travelled to the sixth floor and felt relieved that no one had joined her. She was unsure as to how Michael O'Brien would greet her or react to what she was going to tell him. Colette had decided to confide in him.

"Hello, Colette, how are you feeling?" he asked as she entered his room.

"I'm okay," she replied in a subdued tone, not wishing to get drawn into an unreal conversation about her fictitious illness. "I'm sorry I've been away so long. I'm sorry if I've caused you any problems."

"I was able to get a temporary secretary within a couple of days . . ." he replied. His voice seemed to trail off as if he was going to say something else but had stopped himself.

He gestured to her to sit down and as she did so she felt herself losing her composure. She reached into her bag, pulled out a handkerchief and blew her nose. Michael did not seem to notice. For a moment there was an awkward silence. Then Colette decided to get straight to the point.

"There is something I have to tell you. I haven't been sick. I have a baby – a baby girl. She's just ten months old and she's been given for adoption and I can't get her back," she blurted out, realising that she was not explaining herself very well.

Michael O'Brien looked startled. Before he could ask any questions, she spoke again. This time more slowly, more coherently. For the next half-hour she recounted the whole history of her relationship with Seán Brannigan, the pregnancy, her involvement with St Mark's and her parents' reaction.

"I now definitely want my baby back. The social worker in St Mark's keeps on asking me questions. I know if I go to see her again she will just ask more questions but will not get my baby back for me. She won't help me, my parents won't help me, my room-mate, Sally Thomas, can't help me and I don't want to go near Brannigan."

Michael O'Brien let her talk without interruption. The surprise that had originally registered on his face had now disappeared.

"Why didn't you tell me all of this earlier?" he asked sympathetically.

"I couldn't. We only met a few months ago. I had told nobody and in the beginning I had no reason to tell you because I was certain I wanted my baby adopted. It was only when I saw your sister's baby that I started to have doubts."

"The night you took ill, you mean?"

"Yes, that night."

"Well, why didn't you talk to me or let me in to see you over the last four weeks?"

"I couldn't. I was still trying to keep my secret and sort it out myself. I now realise I can't do it on my own."

"You want my help?" he asked, knowing the answer before she replied that she did. "How can I help?"

"I'm not sure," Colette answered, recognising that she felt a need to unburden herself to him but realising that she did not know what he could do to help her.

"You don't know who the adopters are or where they live?" he asked.

Colette shook her head.

"Well, if the adoption society won't return your baby to you and if you don't know where she is, I think you are going to need a lawyer," he said. "I think I know someone who can help."

He picked up the phone and dialled a number.

"This is Deputy Michael O'Brien speaking. May I have a word with Robert Barnes, please?" There was a pause while he waited. "Hello, Rob, how are you? Good, I'm fine too. I'm phoning you on behalf of my secretary. She has a problem that urgently requires advice and I was hoping you could see her today. That's fine. Three o'clock is okay. See you then. Thanks a lot." He hung up and turned to Colette. "He'll see you at three o'clock," he repeated to her. "Do you want me to come with you?"

"Yes, I would appreciate that," she replied, marvelling at how quickly and practically he had reacted to her story.

* * *

They were sitting in a small room on the second floor of a five-storey office building in Baggot Street. Robert Barnes listened intently as Colette told her story for the second time that day, only interrupting her with the occasional question. As she spoke, he made notes.

Barnes was a tall man of about forty years of age.

He had greeted them in a friendly way at the door of his office. His questions were sympathetic and by the time they were finished Colette felt he was on her side.

"You're quite sure you want Laura back?" he asked her after she had concluded.

"I'm quite sure – absolutely sure."

"If the adopters refuse to return Laura, your only option is to bring court proceedings to get her back and the sooner you do that the better. The longer Laura is with the adopters, the less likely it is that the courts will return her to you."

"You mean, she won't automatically be returned to me?"

"It depends on what view the court takes on Laura's welfare. If you ask the court to return her to you, and the adopters ask that they be allowed to complete the adoption process, the court will decide what should happen on the basis of its view as to what course of action is in the best interests of Laura."

As Robert Barnes spoke, Colette, for the first time since her stay at the Rotunda Hospital, recalled Mrs Comerford saying something similar to her. She now realised that she had not really listened to her on that day or fully digested what she had been told.

"At the time when you agreed to place Laura for adoption, were you not told that if you changed your mind she might not be automatically returned to you, that a court could decide, in the interests of Laura's welfare, that she should remain with the adopters?"

"I was, I think," Colette admitted, "but I gave her to the society only five days after she was born and I don't think I really took it in."

"Well, if we go to court that might help," Barnes commented. "If you are really serious we should get moving quickly."

"I'm really serious."

In Colette's presence a letter was dictated to the adoption society stating that if Laura was not returned to Colette within ten days, court proceedings would issue, seeking a court order granting custody of Laura to Colette.

"If Laura is not returned immediately, and I don't expect she will be, we must make our first court application in two weeks' time," Barnes told her.

* * *

Sitting in Michael O'Brien's car as he drove her back to her flat, Colette felt exhilarated by the speed of events. Her decision was made and things were finally moving. She realised that she should have talked to Michael much earlier but now she hoped that the solicitor's letter would result in Laura being returned. Perhaps Robert Barnes was wrong. Perhaps the adoption society and the adopters would be intimidated by the letter and return Laura to her. By this time next week, she thought, she might be cradling Laura in her arms. A court case might not be necessary at all.

ten

The next day Colette returned to work and, although she had plenty to do that week, the world seemed to go into reverse. She had never known time to pass so slowly. On the Friday night Michael took her out to dinner and they again discussed the events of the previous ten months and Colette's relationship with Seán Brannigan. It was obvious during the meal that Michael had something on his mind, but Colette did not try to find out what it was until the coffee was brought to the table. She felt that if it was important, he would eventually come to it himself. But finally she asked: "What is it, Michael? You look worried about something."

"I got a phone call last night from Robert Barnes and he discussed with me the possible costs of a court case. As a favour to me he will not be looking for legal fees for his work, but he tells me that you probably need two barristers, a senior and junior counsel, and that you may also need the help of a child psychiatrist. He says that all their fees and expenses could come to something in the region of €20,000 and that, if the court hearing were to run for more than three days or if there were to be a Supreme Court appeal, the costs could be considerably greater."

Colette was stunned. She had never really thought about the cost of a court case. All her thoughts had been concentrated on Laura and her desire to get her back.

"I don't have that sort of money. I have about €1000 in savings and I suppose I could get about €5,000 for my car if I sold it. How soon will I need the money?"

"Not for a few weeks," he replied. "If you were unemployed, you would qualify for free legal aid from a government law centre, but because you have a salary, the law centres will not help you. I have been in contact with my bank manager to see if I could increase my loan and get some money together but I am in so much debt from the by-election that he has refused to co-operate."

"I don't want you to give me money; I wouldn't expect that. You've been fantastic already." She wanted to reach out and touch him but was unsure what his reaction would be.

"I don't think you should have to sell your car," he said. "If you succeed in getting Laura back, you're going to need it. I think you should get the money from Brannigan."

"I couldn't . . . wouldn't ask him for anything . . . I don't want anything more to do with him."

"I've been thinking about this all day and I knew you would react in this way. I don't want you to talk to him or have any more contact with him, but I think he owes you something – he can't just turn his back and walk away as if he had no obligations towards you or Laura. I don't want you to ask him for anything. I'll ask him for you."

* * *

Perspiration gathered like tiny globules of rainwater along the lines that ran across Seán Brannigan's brow. He looked like a winded footballer frantically sucking in oxygen to avoid collapse. Michael O'Brien had never before seen a man crumble before his eyes.

"So you know!" Brannigan finally responded in a whispered gasp.

"I know and now she needs your help."

"What help? I heard that she didn't have the child any longer and had given it up for adoption. Her father told me that."

"Her father? When were you talking to her father?"

"He came to see me after he heard she had a baby. He was very distressed. He wanted my help and advice. I pretended I knew nothing of Colette's pregnancy. I told him that she had done the right thing to have the baby adopted."

"Why you? Why did he talk to you when he wouldn't talk to his own daughter?"

"He still doesn't know I am the father," Brannigan replied, grim-faced. "God only knows what he'd do if he found out."

Michael felt the anger burning inside him. "And what about her? What advice did you give about her?"

"I suggested that he should stay away from her for a while . . ." Brannigan started to splutter.

"What else did you tell him?"

"I told him she would eventually realise she had done wrong and when she did, they should forgive her," Brannigan whimpered.

"Jesus, you are some bastard," Michael O'Brien retorted. "You preach morals in this House, get your secretary pregnant and then start moralising with the girl's father. You have some neck. You could at least have encouraged her parents to help her."

Brannigan sat ashen-faced behind his desk and did not reply. At length he looked nervously at Michael O'Brien.

"Have you come here to abuse me or have you some specific proposition in mind?"

Michael O'Brien regretted the way the conversation had developed. He had arranged the meeting to secure financial help for Colette, not to harangue Brannigan. He decided now to come straight to the point.

"Colette gave her baby up for adoption but she

has changed her mind," he explained. "No adoption order has been made yet and she wants the child back. It looks as if the adopters are going to refuse to return the child to her and she may have to go to court. But she doesn't have the money to do so. She needs your help."

"There might be a court case!" Brannigan was aghast. "What does she want me to do? The publicity would finish me. I can't help her in court. It would finish me in politics and wreck my marriage."

"She does not want you in court," O'Brien replied, carefully controlling his distaste. "She just wants you to help to finance the court case. She doesn't have the money to do it all on her own."

Fifteen minutes later Michael O'Brien walked triumphantly out of Seán Brannigan's office. Brannigan remained sitting limply behind his desk. The deal had been done. Brannigan was to forward a cheque for thirty-five thousand euro to Robert Barnes once Barnes had confirmed to him by letter that Colette had issued court proceedings to obtain custody of her daughter. Barnes was also to guarantee that, if she succeeded, she would not claim any money from Brannigan for the child's support. The letter would state that the court case would be heard in private. The press would therefore be excluded and Brannigan's involvement would not become public knowledge. What had clinched the deal was Michael's undertaking that Colette would agree to no publicity.

As he stepped out of the elevator on the ground

floor Michael O'Brien smiled grimly. He had never been in such a situation before and he thought that he had done well. He was pleased that he had got the better of Brannigan, a man whose public pronouncements he had found distasteful long before he had become a member of the Dáil. If Colette had not been involved, he would have liked the court case to get the maximum publicity possible so as to expose Brannigan as a charlatan and a hypocrite. However, it was the promise of no publicity that had secured Brannigan's agreement and committed him to handing over a sum of money that would not only pay for the entire court case but which, Michael hoped, might leave something over at the end for Colette and for her baby daughter.

Michael allowed himself a second smile as he walked into the main entrance hall. He had omitted to tell Brannigan that, whether Colette wished it or not, in Ireland court contests over the custody of children were always heard in private and the press were always excluded. Even if Brannigan had told him to go to hell, not one of Brannigan's constituents would have been able to read a newspaper account of Colette's court case that would have disclosed Brannigan's relationship with Colette and the birth of their child. For a man who regularly made speeches about the sanctity of Irish family life, Brannigan knew surprisingly little about the workings of Irish family law.

eleven

John and Jenny Masterson arrived early and sat quietly in the solicitor's waiting room until the time came for their appointment. They showed no interest in the newspapers or magazines lying on the table. Neither of them talked. Wracked by anxiety, they just sat silently together, surreptitiously holding hands and striving to assemble their thoughts and make some sense of what was happening to them.

John's mind strayed to the previous night. Jenny had cried herself to sleep. On one occasion, hearing her cry out, he had cradled her head on his shoulder and reassured her that she was just dreaming. Kissing her forehead and caressing her cheek as she lay asleep beside him, he started to hate Laura's biological mother, Mrs Gavin and the adoption society for causing Jenny so much pain. He felt angry with himself for his helplessness and his inability to tackle the problem on his own. In his business, he was the decision-maker. A crisis presented an opportunity for action; it was there to be tackled and resolved and he was in command and dominant. In this, he was helpless and dependent on others. It was a family crisis that he could not confront and solve on his own.

John lay restlessly in bed, unable to sleep. Getting out of bed, he wandered into Laura's room and stood staring at her as she slept peacefully in her cot. He wanted to lift her and hold her close to him, to kiss her little puckered lips and flat nose and rub her hair against his cheek. Not for the first time he noticed her special smell, the smell that attaches to all cleanly scrubbed and powdered babies but he thought it unique and special to her. He reached down to touch her but stopped, afraid he would wake her. Instead he stood in the dark staring at her, terrified that she would be taken from them and afraid that he might one day forget what she looked like. He then slowly walked downstairs into the lounge, sat on the sofa and cried.

Jenny had been through so much and what was happening now was so unfair. For three years before the decision to adopt had been taken, their lovemaking had been dominated by dates and thermometers. They had both become so anxious for Jenny to conceive that all spontaneity had been lost. John had started to dread those occasions when she would phone his office in the middle of the day to tell him that the optimum time had arrived, and he would have to rush home to make love during the lunch-hour. This feeling of dread made him feel guilty as he knew it was all much worse for Jenny than for himself. As each monthly cycle ended and nature took its course, the renewed look of despair in Jenny's eyes reflected the tension and distress they both felt. No other communication was necessary between them.

With Laura's arrival all had changed utterly. It was like being back in the early months of their marriage. Making love had ceased to be a duty and had again become a celebration. It was now not only a celebration of their love for each other but of their love for Laura.

"Mr and Mrs Masterson."

Their names being called interrupted his train of thought.

Jenny spoke first. "Yes?"

"Mr Galloway will see you now," the young receptionist in the yellow blouse said to them.

They were shown into an imposing room dominated by massive green and brown law volumes on bookshelves that covered the walls.

A youngish-looking red-haired man came out from behind a large desk. He shook their hands and gestured towards two chairs.

Paul Galloway was thirty-five years of age and married with two children. He had been a practising solicitor for about ten years and was relatively well-known as an expert on family law. He was not popular and was viewed with a certain degree of antagonism by colleagues in the legal profession. This was because he regularly crossed the legal boundaries that divided solicitors and barristers by undertaking his own advocacy work in the Irish superior courts, in particular the High Court. By doing so he had won a number of major cases and had achieved considerable public notoriety. It was Mrs Gavin who had suggested Paul Galloway's name to the Mastersons the night before, and early that morning John had phoned his office for an urgent appointment.

"I understand from my secretary that you have a child placed with you for adoption, a baby girl, and that the child's mother has changed her mind and wants her daughter returned to her," Galloway said.

"Yes, that's the situation," John replied. "Until last night we thought everything was going smoothly and that the Adoption Authority would make an adoption order within the next three to four weeks. Now the mother's solicitor has written to the adoption society requesting that Laura be returned to her."

"Do you have a copy of this letter?" Galloway asked.

"No, we were told of it by Mrs Gavin, our social worker. We have come to see you because we don't know what to do next. We don't want to lose her."

"I see," Galloway replied. "First I would like to get some more background information from you. Then I will discuss the legal position and suggest what should now be done."

John outlined the family history, describing in

detail Laura's development during the ten months she had lived with them and the various interviews with Mrs Gavin and Imelda Hennessy. Then he went on to relate the events of the previous evening.

"We don't want to give Laura back," he concluded emphatically.

While John was speaking, Jenny had sat silently beside him.

"Can you help us?" she now asked plaintively.

Galloway, understanding their anxiety, tried to put them at ease.

"I'll do everything possible to help you to keep Laura," he replied. "What did the social worker – Mrs Gavin – say when you told her you wished to keep Laura?"

"She said the society would write to the mother's solicitor and tell him how we felt," John replied. "She explained that neither she nor the adoption society had any power to remove Laura from us and had no intention of doing so and that the next move would be up to the mother. She also suggested we should come to you for legal help."

For the first time Galloway smiled.

"If the mother sticks to her decision, it is up to her to start court proceedings to regain custody. If her solicitor is efficient he could obtain an initial court order to get the proceedings underway within a few days. However, in this situation, many mothers just sit back and do nothing."

"What should we do at this stage?" John asked.

"Absolutely nothing," Galloway replied. "Laura has been with you for over ten months. The longer she is with you before a custody conflict comes before the courts, the better. The greater the time she is in your care, the more secure your position becomes."

"We just sit back and wait for the blow to strike?" John asked incredulously.

"That's more or less it. If the mother starts a custody case, we then reply by issuing adoption proceedings against her and ask the court to dispense with or waive her consent so that the adoption process can be completed and an adoption order made without the necessity of her co-operation. The court will hear both applications together and make its decision on the basis of what course of action should be favoured to protect Laura's welfare. To succeed, we must not only prove that Laura has no relationship with her biological mother; we must also convince the court that Laura regards you as her *real* parents, that she has bonded to both of you and is attached to other members of your family. The longer she is with you, the deeper the bonds. The deeper the bonds, the less inclined the courts are to break them."

"What happens if the mother does nothing? What do we do if she simply withholds her consent so that no adoption order can be made, but does not do anything more to get Laura back?" John asked.

"If that happens, we just sit tight and wait until Laura has been with you for a minimum of eighteen months, or longer if possible, if you can live with it. Then we bring our own adoption case. You leave it as long as you can, so that when it comes to court there is very little room for a judge to doubt that Laura's welfare demands that a decision be made in your favour."

"Do you mean we hang around in a sort of limbo waiting for time to pass?"

"Well, if you don't, if you rush into court, the court may take the view that any harm that would be caused to Laura by her being removed from both of you would be offset by the advantage to her of being brought up by her biological mother. For example, if we were heading into a court hearing tomorrow morning, your possibilities of success would be much less than if we were involved in a court contest this time next year. If we were in court tomorrow or next week, it is probable that a judge would be inclined to find in favour of the biological mother and would order that Laura be returned to her."

* * *

The Mastersons were both dazed as they left Galloway's office. It had been agreed that they would simply sit back and do nothing. They had been reassured that no social worker could call to their home and demand that Laura be returned. If they received any letters or court papers, they were to contact Galloway immediately. As they turned into the driveway of her sister's home to collect Laura, Jenny realised that it was still only twelve forty-five.

Less than twenty-four hours had passed since Mrs Gavin had phoned and arranged to visit to tell them of the mother's change of mind. In those twenty-four hours John and Jenny's world had been turned upside down.

twelve

After their visit to Galloway, John and Jenny found it extremely difficult to settle back into their normal routine. At work John lost all powers of concentration. Seated at the circular conference table in his spacious office overlooking St Stephen's Green, he rushed through the early morning strategy meetings with his assistants every day, knowing that he could rely on their experience and expertise to keep the business going. Formulating an advertising campaign to promote sales of a new brand of toothpaste or to increase the market share of a well-known biscuit company seemed so trivial when compared to the struggle with which he and Jenny were confronted. Even the finalising of a series of proposals for a political party explaining how best to get its message across to the electorate could not arouse John's interest, although he had been something of an armchair politician for many years. Laura dominated his thoughts and he was consumed by a fear that she would be taken away. He constantly asked himself why this was happening to them. What could he do to protect Laura? What would happen to them if Laura's mother succeeded in taking her from them? What would happen to Laura?

* * *

Alone in the house with Laura, Jenny's heart missed a beat every time the phone rang or doorbell chimed, in fear that the caller might bring bad news. Most of the phone calls were from John, checking that everything was alright, the rest mainly from Jenny's sister Ruth. On the morning they had arranged to see Galloway, they had told Ruth what was happening and made her promise that she would tell no one else except her husband, David, as they did not want sympathy calls from their entire family. Since then David and Ruth had visited them regularly and she and John were glad to have their company. At night when Laura was asleep in her cot, Jenny and John found themselves going into her room to check that she was still there, that she had not been taken from them. It became a nightly ritual. At two or three o'clock in the morning, waking from a light sleep, Jenny would slip out of bed, anxious not to disturb John, and sneak into Laura's room to find John already standing there.

During the day, Jenny would not go anywhere without Laura. No longer would she leave her with

Ruth while she went shopping in the supermarket. At night, she and John stayed at home, not wishing to leave Laura with baby-sitters. If Laura awoke from her sleep, they both wanted to be there to reassure her that they would always be there, and to convince each other that she would always be there.

Ten days after Mrs Gavin's visit to their home, Jenny phoned St Mark's to find out whether they had heard any more from the mother or her solicitor.

"The morning after I saw you and John the society wrote to the mother's solicitor telling him that you were unwilling to return Laura to her. We have received no further letter from him."

"Has the girl not even been in contact with the society?"

"No, she hasn't, she has made no contact with us at all."

When nearly five weeks had passed since Mrs Gavin's visit and they had heard nothing more from Laura's biological mother, some of their anxiety lifted. John and Jenny finally started to plan for Christmas, which was only ten days away. They reassured each other that everything would be alright.

"The more time that passes, the more secure your position becomes," Galloway had said, and each week that passed the Mastersons grew more confident that Laura would remain with them.

Christmas was a time of celebration. All their anxiety about Laura seemed to vanish. When they visited relations and friends, she was the centre of attention.

Everyone marvelled at how big she had grown – at the blondeness of her hair, the blueness of her eyes, her likeness to Jenny. She was no longer crawling, but walking now and into everything.

Rebel followed her wherever she went, like a toy dog on a string. They played a new game. She would stand beside him and he would nuzzle her tummy and gently push her into a sitting position on the floor. She would then stand up and the process would start all over again. The dog's tail wagged so fast that it looked in danger of breaking off, while Laura's giggles would grow into uncontrollable laughter until tears of delight ran down her tiny red cheeks.

Ruth and David remained the only members of the family who knew of recent events and, as a result, the "hassle" as they called it, was not a topic of family conversation and only once spoiled the Christmas festivities. On Christmas Day, after they had all finished the turkey and plum pudding, in Jenny's parents' home, Jenny's mother, holding Laura on her knee, talked of how big she had grown and how lucky they were to adopt such a beautiful baby.

"The adoption order should be made fairly soon," she said, more by way of a statement than a question.

"Yes, we hope so," said John before Jenny could reply, casting a nervous glance in his wife's direction. He quickly diverted the conversation but was nonetheless conscious of the vacant look that appeared on Jenny's face and the sadness in her eyes. Like him, she was still terrified that Laura would be taken from them and that no adoption order would ever be made. John wondered about Laura's biological mother (he always thought of her as "the biological mother" as if the phrase signified something different from a real mother): What was she doing, why had they heard no more from her, why had she not gone to court? He prayed that she had changed her mind, that after Christmas she would give her consent and that all the worry and uncertainty would end. He looked again at Jenny, brown eyes meeting blue eyes in unspoken conversation. Simultaneously they smiled and reached for each other's hand across the table, each silently acknowledging and understanding the other's thoughts and fears.

* * *

Colette lay in the hospital bed and gazed out the window. Snowflakes were falling gently out of a grey winter sky and the world had turned white. She shifted position and felt a stabbing pain break through the dull ache in the centre of her stomach. The next time she moved more carefully. She had been in hospital for almost four weeks but was going home tomorrow. Her parents had insisted that she go home to them and she had agreed. Sally Thomas was going to stay with her parents in Ballina and the flat would be empty.

Four weeks earlier, Colette had found both her parents sitting beside her bed when she awoke from the anaesthetic: her father contrite, begging for her forgiveness and praying she would recover; her mother weeping hysterically. Initially she was confused. Thinking that she had just given birth, she wondered how they knew since she had never told them she was pregnant. She tried to move, to push her body upwards with her elbows into a sitting position and gasped, suddenly conscious of the agonising pain. Her insides felt on fire. Then she remembered stepping out of bed that morning and collapsing onto the floor; the sound of a siren; nurses rushing her out of the ambulance and a man in a white coat injecting her arm. Moving her hand slowly down the front of her body, she found a large bandage at the point where the pain hurt most.

"Thank God you're going to be alright." It was her mother's voice breaking through the tears.

"What happened?"

"A burst appendix," her father answered. "Take it easy, don't try and sit up. You've had an operation, but you're going to be okay."

Sally had phoned her parents from the hospital while Colette was on the operating table. They had visited her every day, sometimes twice a day, and the reconciliation was now complete.

The morning she collapsed Colette was to have gone to Robert Barnes' office to sign the papers that would start the court proceedings to regain custody of Laura. It was intended that the first court application would be made within a couple of days of her signing. Then everything had been postponed until after Christmas and the papers would have to be redrafted before she could sign them. The application originally stated that if Laura was returned to Colette she would live with her in the flat with Sally Thomas and that Sally would be available to help with Laura's day-to-day care. But now the court papers would say that Colette had the full backing and support of her parents, Laura's grandparents, and that, if Laura was returned to her, she and Laura would live with them. This would offer Laura the opportunity to live with and be brought up by not only her real mother but also her real grandparents.

Twelve days after Christmas, sitting in her father's car on the drive back from Robert Barnes' office, Colette thought to herself that the operation and extra delay might ultimately prove helpful. Surely now, she thought, she was more likely to succeed, more likely to be able to convince the court that it was very much in Laura's best interest that she be returned to the custody and care of her real mother.

thirteen

"Hello, is John or Jenny there, please?"

Jenny immediately recognised the voice at the other end of the phone.

"Jenny speaking. Good afternoon, Miss Hennessy."

"Good afternoon, I'm phoning you about Laura. I want to call over to see you and John this evening. Is that alright?"

"Of course it is," Jenny heard herself replying automatically. "What's wrong? Has anything happened?"

"I'm afraid the Adoption Authority was served with the court papers just a short time ago and I have to give copies of them to you. The mother wants Laura back."

Jenny quickly ended the conversation and phoned John. She tried to sound calm but broke down and sobbed into the phone. He spoke to her quietly, lovingly trying to reassure her, wishing he felt as confident of their winning their court case as he sounded, wishing someone would reassure him.

As he put the phone down John realised that decisions were going to be made by others that would affect him and Jenny and that what he did or said would not necessarily be the deciding factor. He was used to being in command and for the first time he felt he was losing control over his own life. Immediately he phoned Galloway and told him what was happening and the solicitor arranged to see them both the next morning. Then he drove home to Jenny and Laura.

* * *

"The mother wants Laura back." Those words echoed and re-echoed inside Jenny's head as she mechanically prepared the evening meal, waiting for John to arrive home.

"Doesn't she care about Laura, about what she wants?" She was speaking to herself now, as she stood looking out into the garden through the kitchen window, tears streaming down her face. She wanted to scream or hit out at something. It was all so unfair. She remembered throwing a tantrum years ago as a schoolgirl and arguing with her own mother about something long forgotten and now, fifteen years later, she felt herself losing control as she had done on that occasion. Turning from the window she saw a basin of wet clothes in the middle of the kitchen floor. Basin and clothes parted company as she kicked it viciously. Wet underwear and towels shot through the air in all directions and the basin crashed against a kitchen cupboard. A milk carton toppled and fell off the counter, spilling its contents all over the floor. A baby shrieked. With a start Jenny remembered that Laura had settled down for her afternoon sleep half an hour before Miss Hennessy's phone call. She had slept peacefully until then.

Jenny quickly went into her bedroom and lifted her out of the cot. The crying stopped instantly and was replaced with cheerful gurgling as Jenny wiped Laura's eyes and cheeks with a tissue.

Carrying Laura into the kitchen, she was shocked to see the havoc she had created. She felt ashamed that she had lost her self-control but she also felt better, as if she had got something out of her system. As Laura sat in her baby chair sucking at a piece of bread, Jenny rapidly tidied up. She knew that John would be halfway home by now and she didn't want him to see the mess. As she put the last wet towel back into the basin, she heard a familiar voice.

"Ma-ma, Ma-ma," the voice said and she turned around and looked at Laura. Two little arms reached out towards Jenny from the high chair. "Ma-ma, Ma-ma," Laura repeated as she was unstrapped and lifted out of the chair. "Ma-ma, Ma-ma," she said again as Jenny held her close, stroking her soft blonde hair with her right hand as Laura's chin nuzzled into her shoulder. Jenny knew that to Laura she was her real mother, her only mother. She needed and wanted no other mother. Holding Laura between her two hands at head height and looking straight into her blue eyes, Jenny whispered: "I love you, Daddy loves you and Rebel loves you. Imelda Hennessy says your mother wants you back but as far as you and I are concerned I am your mother, you are my baby girl and no one is going to take you away from here."

Jenny held Laura close to her again and kissed the back of her neck. Appreciating the solemnity of the moment, Laura again gurgled.

"Ma-ma, Ma-ma," she repeated and then threw up, sending a white stream of chewed bread running down the back of Jenny's neck.

* * *

Imelda Hennessy appeared cold and unsympathetic. Speaking in a matter-of-fact voice, she explained that the court papers required the Mastersons to produce Laura in the High Court in six days' time. To their surprise, she was not sure whether this meant they had actually to bring Laura into court or whether it was just a procedural device to get the court proceedings under way. If they wished to keep Laura and contest the case, they should immediately see a lawyer. The Adoption Authority could do nothing to help them and she could not give them any other advice. She and the Adoption Authority had to remain completely neutral.

John and Jenny sat in their lounge listening quietly to her. They had both hoped that the day would never arrive when they would have to become embroiled in court proceedings, but now it had and they were prepared to face the challenge.

"I understand from Mrs Gavin in St Mark's that you intend to oppose the mother?" Imelda Hennessy said with apparent indifference.

"Yes, that's right," replied Jenny, feeling no obligation to say any more or to give any explanation to this cold and distant women who, she suspected, was enjoying her dramatic visit and was being deliberately unhelpful.

Imelda Hennessy left within fifteen minutes of arriving, depositing the court papers on their hall table. John and Jenny read through them, immediately noticing that all references to the mother's name and to her residential and work addresses were illegible, covered by thick black marker to preserve her anonymity. They both read the synopsis of the mother's story – unmarried, 21 years old, father of child a married man, employed as his secretary, parents unaware of pregnancy, uncertain what to do, agreeing to adoption three days after child's birth, signing the papers two days later, wanting child back, parents now supportive, longing for child, child not seen by her since birth.

To her surprise Jenny realised that her anger was subsiding and being replaced by a feeling of sadness. Until that moment the "biological mother" had never been a real person to her, a human being with flesh and emotions. She had merely been an object towards whom she had conflicting feelings. Initially, she had been grateful to this unknown person for allowing her to become a mother but was also envious of her fertility and her capacity to carry a growing baby inside her. Later this gratitude had been replaced by a bitter resentment and fear: resentment that the biological mother could want to take back Laura after abandoning her so quickly after birth and fear that she might succeed, depriving her and John of the baby they both loved so much and separating Laura from the only parents she had ever known. The mother had now established herself as a real person and Jenny knew her story and understood her behaviour in a way she had not done until then. She knew how desolate she and John would feel if Laura was taken from them and thought she understood how this young mother must feel having seen her child only once, a few minutes after its birth. Jenny felt a deep sense of compassion which she immediately knew she had to overcome. She and John had to be strong to fight their battle and they had to win. They had to defeat this young mother's opposition to their adopting her child, although Jenny knew the bitterness she had felt towards the mother was now gone and would not return. The other woman was no longer an object of hatred. Jenny wanted to reach out to her, to explain why she and John had to oppose her, had to fight her tooth and nail. She hoped that at the end of it all they would not become hate figures to her, that if they won she would one day forgive them and that she would understand that their determination to oppose her derived from their love for Laura.

* * *

They did not have to produce Laura in court. Galloway explained that this was just a legal device to ensure that the court proceedings were processed quickly. The court case would be heard in about six to eight weeks' time and they must now institute their own court action, asking the court to permit them to keep Laura and to allow the Adoption Authority to make an adoption order, despite the mother's opposition. They followed Galloway's advice. Court papers were prepared and signed by both of them. Then, accompanied by Laura, they went to the child guidance unit in St James's Hospital for assessment to enable the child psychiatrist there, a Dr O'Connell, to prepare a welfare report for the court proceedings and to give evidence in court. At the request of the mother's lawyer they agreed to a second assessment being carried out by a Dr Lloyd, a child psychiatrist attached to St Brigid's Hospital, so that a second welfare report could be prepared and the evidence of another child psychiatrist made available to assist the court in deciding Laura's future.

Dr O'Connell arranged to call on the Mastersons at home twelve days after their visit to her. One Sunday afternoon she arrived. It had been agreed that Ruth and David would also be present and unexpectedly Jenny's parents called in. Dr O'Connell was introduced to Jenny's parents as a friend of John's – they were still unaware of what was happening. Later on that evening John and Jenny agreed that they would have to be told, so that they could prepare themselves for the possibility of things going wrong.

Dr O'Connell forwarded her report to Galloway a week later and referred to the Mastersons as a tightly knit happy family unit within which Laura had formed all her bonds and attachments. John and Jenny were described as Laura's "psychological parents". Even Rebel received an unexpected and honourable mention as the "beloved dog".

By the time John and Jenny received a copy of the report from Galloway they had broken the news to Jenny's parents. To everyone's surprise they announced that they had "suspected there was a problem" as the adoption of Kate and Arthur's baby – friends of John and Jenny – had been completed much more quickly. They offered to give evidence in court if necessary. Because of the glowing reference to them in Dr O'Connell's report, their offer was quickly accepted.

fourteen

After her discharge from hospital, Colette returned to live in her parents' home. Sally and her father moved her clothes and other belongings out of the flat and she tried to settle into a routine. She returned to work for Michael O'Brien and they spent the occasional evening together discussing the forthcoming court case over a drink or a meal. While the preliminary legal work was being done, she tried to put it all to the back of her mind and was able to do so for two or three days in a row. It would then suddenly engulf her and for days she would be unable to think or talk of anything else.

Tossing and turning in bed at night, she was tormented by distorted images of Laura as a new-born baby. In her nightmare she was under cross-examination in the witness box and had no convincing answers to any of the questions she was asked. Why do you want your child back? Why did you give her away? Why have you changed your mind? What sort of a mother would you make? Her head pounding, she would wake up, soaked in perspiration.

When Colette met Robert Barnes he was always cautious about the outcome of the case and she could not make up her mind whether he genuinely thought she might lose or whether he was trying to ensure that she did not take it for granted that she would succeed.

In the middle of February, five weeks after the court proceedings had been initiated, Colette received a letter from Mrs Comerford telling her that if she wished to call in to see her at St Mark's to discuss the general situation, she would do whatever she could to help her. She had no great desire to meet this woman again but Barnes advised her to make an appointment since he had no doubt that she would be called as a witness in the court hearing. It was important, he advised Colette, that Mrs Comerford should paint a favourable picture of her when giving her evidence.

* * *

Parking her car outside St Mark's, Colette shivered. She felt threatened by the building and its occupants and knew she had to be careful about what she said. She walked slowly up the steps and rang the bell. The door was swiftly opened and she was taken straight in to see Mrs Comerford without having to sit in the waiting room first.

"Hello, Colette, how are you?" Mrs Comerford asked, extending her hand in a friendly greeting.

Taken aback by the other woman's warmth, Colette automatically took her hand.

"Please sit down."

Colette sank back into an armchair and Mrs Comerford sat on a chair beside her.

"Well, you have made your decision that you definitely want Laura back?"

"Yes, that's right," Colette responded quickly, anxious to emphasise her commitment, "and now it's all up to the court to decide what's going to happen."

"I want you to know that no matter what decision the court makes, I'll give you all the support I can and I want you to feel free to ask for help or call in for a chat if you need someone to talk to. I understand what you're going through, although it may not appear like that to you, and I don't want you to think we are on opposite sides."

Colette had not slept on the night before this meeting, because she was so afraid of what this woman might say to her and so nervous as to how she might react. She had seen her as a threatening figure and held her responsible for Laura being with adopters. Now she remembered that right at the start, Mrs Comerford had cautioned her against agreeing too soon to Laura's adoption but she had ignored her advice.

"I want so much to see Laura," Colette explained. "You were right when you told me to see her again before she went to adopters. If I had taken your advice I'm sure I would have kept her and none of this would have happened."

"Would you like the society to ask the adopters whether they would be willing to bring Laura here so that you could see her?" Mrs Comerford asked. "I don't know whether they would agree, but they might."

"Do you really think they might?" Colette was incredulous. "Of course I'd love to see her, but I never imagined it would be possible before the court hearing. Wouldn't their solicitor tell them not to co-operate or agree to such a request?"

"I really don't know, but I can find out if you want me to."

"I can't tell you how much I want to see Laura, to see how she's grown, what she looks like now. Please, Mrs Comerford, do try and arrange it!"

Colette left St Mark's elated. It had never occurred to her that there was a possibility of her seeing Laura again unless she won in court. When she had arrived three-quarters of an hour earlier she had been anxious to make an impression, to ensure that Mrs Comerford understood the extent of her commitment to recover Laura, worried that she might say something that could be repeated in the witness box as evidence against her. Mrs Comerford had been an enemy to appease. She had now become an ally, willing to give whatever assistance she could when requested to do so by Colette. Maybe everything would turn out alright after all, she thought, as she drove home.

fifteen

They always read each other's mail. This particular letter was addressed to both of them, Jenny noticed, as she tore the envelope open. She immediately recognised the St Mark's motif on the top of the page and her heart skipped a beat. Was it possible that the mother had changed her mind again and was now consenting? Her hopes immediately evaporated as she read the letter's contents. It asked whether they would be willing to bring Laura along to the society on a convenient afternoon so that the mother could see her. It emphasised that this was a request made on behalf of the mother and suggested that "in the light of existing court proceedings" they should obtain legal advice prior to replying. The letter concluded by expressing a hope that they would feel able to comply with the mother's request since "she has not seen her child since the day it was born".

John finished showering and came down for breakfast as Jenny was feeding rusks to Laura. She handed him the letter to a refrain of "Da-da, Da-da" from the baby chair.

"Why are they suggesting this now?" she asked.

"I don't know. I think I should phone Paul Galloway straight after breakfast."

"Do you think they want us to meet the mother or that they only want Laura to meet her?"

"I really don't know what they have in mind. What would you like to do, Jenny? Would you like to go along to this kind of meeting?"

"In some ways I wouldn't mind. Don't you wonder sometimes what the mother looks like, what sort of person she is?"

"I suppose our meeting her or her seeing Laura after all this time can't do any harm," John said thoughtfully. "But we shouldn't do anything without talking to Paul Galloway first."

Breakfast over, John phoned Galloway's office, knowing that he always started work early. He read the letter over the phone and told Galloway that they were prepared to agree to the mother's request and that they were willing to meet her with Laura, but wanted to know exactly what was to happen at the meeting and who else was going to be there.

"I don't think there's any harm in such a meeting taking place if you are willing to go along with it," Paul Galloway advised. "In fact it might even be helpful in relation to the court hearing."

He offered to phone the society to get further information.

Twenty minutes after John had arrived at his office, Paul Galloway was on the phone to him again.

"The meeting with the mother is to take place on Wednesday at St Mark's. Your social worker and the mother's social worker will be present throughout the meeting and false names will be used so that you do not discover each other's true identity. The meeting is to last for approximately half an hour but can be shorter, depending on how it goes. It has been scheduled for two o'clock in the afternoon. Is there any other information that you want or anything else I can do to help?"

"You're quite sure that it's alright? What happens if the mother holds Laura and makes some scene and refuses to hand her back?"

"There is no problem there. The society has her agreement that she will co-operate fully with you and there will be no question of her behaving in that way. I'm told that she'll be delighted and surprised that you're agreeing to allow her to see Laura – she didn't believe you would."

* * *

They arrived at St Mark's at 1.50 p.m. As John parked the car he wondered whether the mother was already inside. Laura was sitting in her car-seat next to Jenny in the back. "Ma-ma, Ma-ma," she kept repeating, holding tightly onto a soft pink elephant that she had received from "Granna" for her birthday four weeks earlier. Once inside St Mark's, the Mastersons were first taken into Mrs Gavin's room.

"How are you both?" she asked, her hand clasping John's hand and shaking it warmly as Jenny held firmly onto Laura. "Do sit down. You're both so very good to come and agree to allow the mother to meet Laura."

"I hope we're doing the right thing," Jenny said.

"I have no doubt you are, no doubt at all. Now, I'm going to introduce you to the mother as Colin and Jackie. I hope those names are alright? We are anxious to preserve your anonymity and Laura will be called 'Baby', although she really is not a baby any longer, are you, Laura?"

Laura did not even look up. She was engrossed in her game with the elephant, bouncing it up and down along the arm of the chair on which Jenny was sitting.

"If you're ready and there's nothing you wish to ask me, we'll go ahead. The mother has been here since around one thirty and I don't want to prolong the agony for everyone."

*　*　*

On her arrival at St Mark's Colette had immediately been ushered into Mrs Comerford's room. As they awaited Laura's arrival, Mrs Comerford had tried to engage her in small-talk but she found it difficult to respond, and found herself constantly glancing up at the clock in the corner of the room. At last she heard the knock on the door. Her heart started to pound more loudly and quickly.

"Come in, please," Mrs Comerford said.

Three adults entered the room: two women and a man who was carrying a small girl in his arms. Colette sat glued to her seat, staring at the little girl she had been told to call "Baby", realising that she was no longer a baby. The child's size troubled Colette. She knew that Laura was now over thirteen months old and understood that she would have grown. Mrs Comerford had even mentioned this whilst they were waiting for the others to arrive, but Colette had never been able to conceptualise the growing process. In her daydreams and nightmares Laura had always appeared as the tiny body that lay beside her in the delivery room, a small shrivelled baby wrapped in a pink sheet. The child she was now looking at bore no resemblance to the baby that had dominated her thoughts and taken over her life in the preceding month. The door closed and she heard a voice as if from a distance.

"Anne, this is Jackie and Colin and Baby, together with Mrs Gavin from St Mark's."

Remembering that Anne was her pseudonym for the day, Colette responded. Standing up she held out her hand to each of the adults. As they went through the formalities of being introduced, Colette continued to stare at Laura. She had thick blonde hair and blue eyes, puckered lips and flat pug nose. Momentarily her gaze fixed on the nose. For the first time in months an image of Brannigan flashed into her mind. She recognised the nose but couldn't understand why she wished it was shaped differently.

"I hope we didn't keep you waiting too long," John said, trying to cut through the tension.

"No, I was very early," Colette replied, still staring at Laura. "She's so big!"

"Yes, she grows out of everything so quickly," Jenny responded.

The conversation was stilted and difficult.

"You have dressed her so beautifully," Colette remarked.

"She's not always so clean-looking. She gets into everything!"

They sat down in a circle of armchairs and the small talk continued. Questions were asked, replies given, comments made, but all the time Colette's eyes and thoughts concentrated on Laura as she fought to absorb the change in her appearance and to replace the image she had clung to for over a year of an hour-old baby.

Laura quietly moved over from John's to Jenny's lap and sat, clutching the pink elephant, her eyes darting around the room and taking in the strange surroundings and the faces of the new people. After a few minutes she lost interest and restarted her game, bouncing the elephant along the arm of the chair in which Jenny was sitting.

The conversation stopped and they all remained a moment in silence, looking at one another. Mrs Comerford intervened for the first time.

"Should we all have some tea?" Before anyone could reply she had lifted the telephone and requested tea for all of them.

For the first time Jenny recognised her as the woman who had accompanied Mrs Gavin on one of her early visits to their home. When she had been introduced to her earlier, Jenny had thought her face was familiar but could not recall where they had previously met.

As Mrs Comerford's short phone conversation ended and before the room again became silent, Colette forced herself to speak.

"Do you think I could hold her?" she asked awkwardly, looking straight at Jenny, uncertain of her reaction.

Jenny did not reply. She just stood up and quickly carried Laura over to Colette, who remained seated. As Laura was placed on Colette's lap she held tightly on to her elephant and chatted away to it. It was as if she had not even noticed the change in the seating arrangement.

"Hello, Baby," Colette said self-consciously, speaking as quietly and as tenderly as possible.

Laura looked up at Colette, acknowledging for the first time that she was sitting somewhere different.

"Hello, Baby," Colette repeated, feeling herself

blushing as all eyes in the room concentrated on her and Laura. She had tried to envisage what it would be like to hold her daughter close to her again and had secretly hoped for a moment such as this. Her prayers now answered, she realised that she was not enjoying the experience and felt increasingly uncomfortable at being the centre of attention.

"That's a lovely elephant," she said soothingly, taking it gently from Laura's hand. She knew instantly that she had made a mistake. Laura screamed and the spell was broken. Colette pressed the pink toy back into Laura's hand but the child was crying hysterically now.

"Ma-ma, Ma-ma!" she cried, reaching out to Jenny.

"It's okay, it's okay," Colette muttered, panic-stricken by Laura's cries. She leaned forward to kiss Laura on the back of her neck but as she did so Laura's left hand swung back and struck her on the cheek.

Jenny lifted Laura from Colette's lap and stood in the middle of the room, cradling her in her arms.

"I am sorry, I didn't mean that to happen. I didn't want to upset her," Colette said, looking frantically towards Mrs Comerford for help.

Jenny felt her composure slipping.

"If you don't want her upset, why are you trying to take her away from us? Why don't you just leave us alone and let an adoption order be made?" she blurted out, regretting what she was saying even as she spoke the words.

At that moment the door opened and there was a

rattle of cups. A tray with a pot of tea and biscuits was put on the table by the elderly receptionist.

Miraculously, Laura stopped crying. "Bickie, bickie," she shouted, immediately distracted, and pointed to the plate piled high with biscuits.

Jenny bent down, picked up a biscuit and handed it to Laura and then settled back in her seat with Laura again sitting quietly on her lap. The elephant was now forgotten, lying on the floor at Jenny's feet, and Laura concentrated on licking the chocolate off the top of the biscuit that had been handed to her.

"I'll pour the tea," announced Mrs Gavin, making her first contribution to the gathering.

"I really didn't mean to upset her," Colette explained hurriedly.

"I'm sorry, I shouldn't have spoken to you like that," Jenny replied, "but this is really difficult for all of us. I hope you understand."

Laura sat on Jenny's lap happily chewing at the biscuit, cheerfully oblivious of the tension all around her. The biscuit broke in two. She held a piece in each hand and examined them quizzically. Then, leaning forward, she handed a piece of biscuit to Colette.

"Thank you," Colette said, taking the biscuit in her hand.

Laura held out her hand again and Colette handed the biscuit back to her. A game developed and the biscuit got passed backwards and forwards as everyone drank their cup of tea. Each time Colette handed the biscuit back to her, Laura giggled with delight and immediately returned the biscuit to Colette. The atmosphere became more relaxed.

"You work as a secretary, I understand," Jenny said tentatively.

"Yes, that's right," Colette replied, not taking her eyes off Laura as she handed back the biscuit for the ninth time. "Do you work?" she asked Jenny automatically to keep the conversation going.

"I used to, but not any more. Looking after Laura is a full-time occupation." As she completed the sentence Jenny realised that she had made a mistake. She had accidentally revealed Laura's name. Feeling uneasy again, she lapsed into silence.

Colette was startled by the woman's reference to Laura's name. How could she know the name Colette had given her? The adopters could never have named her Laura as well – that would have been too much of a coincidence. Perhaps someone in the adoption society had told them by mistake. She wondered what else they had been told.

The game with Laura continued and the giggling had now changed to laughter.

"Do you think I could hold her again?" Colette asked pleadingly, looking straight at Jenny, fearful that she would say no.

"Do you think that would be wise?" John asked Mrs Gavin, doubt registering on his face.

"I think she is more used to me now," Colette said, less unsure of herself. "Just for a few minutes, please. I may never see her again after today."

John glanced at Jenny.

"Just for a couple of minutes," Jenny said, before Mrs Gavin had time to reply to John's question. Jenny leaned forward to pass Laura over to Colette but, as she did so, Laura sensed what was about to happen, wrapped her arms tightly round Jenny's neck and started to whimper.

"I'm sorry, I don't think it will work," Jenny said, letting Laura settle down again on her lap.

"I think perhaps we should go now," John intervened quickly.

"I think so too," agreed Jenny, anxious to leave St Mark's and to bring this increasingly painful meeting to a close.

They all stood up and shook hands again.

"May I kiss her goodbye?" Colette asked, fighting back the tears.

Jenny held Laura as Colette leaned forward, kissing her on the cheek, lingering for a moment to feel Laura's soft smooth skin against her lips. A tear ran down Colette's cheek.

"You have both looked after her so well. Thank you for agreeing to let me see her."

"Do we all have to go to court? Is there no other way?" John's voice trailed off, his eyes concentrating on the distraught face of the pretty blonde girl who had given birth to his daughter.

"I don't know . . . I need more time to think . . ."

"I think we should definitely bring our get-together to an end," interrupted Mrs Comerford as she guided

John and Jenny to the door. Mrs Gavin quickly accompanied them.

Colette felt helpless as she watched Laura disappear out of the room in Jenny's arms. The room was quiet now and Mrs Comerford came back and gestured to her to sit down again. Colette felt totally drained and confused. She wanted Laura back but realised how difficult it would be to handle her and she recognised that, as far as Laura was concerned, the adopters were her parents and she was just a stranger. Yet there had been some recognition. Surely she wouldn't have played the biscuit game so readily with a complete stranger? Surely this was a sign of something?

"They've looked after her well, haven't they?" she heard Mrs Comerford say, her voice interrupting her thoughts.

"Yes, I suppose so."

"She's a beautiful baby – a credit to all of you."

"Yes, I suppose she is. Mrs Comerford, what am I do? I want her back so much but I still have doubts. What should I do?"

"I can't tell you what to do. You must make your own decision. If I told you what I thought now, I could be accused by the courts or the lawyers of trying to influence you. If you are not sure what you want, the courts will ultimately make the decision for all of you on the basis of what is best for Laura."

"I felt so awkward holding her on my lap. I wasn't quite sure what I should do with her."

"I would have been surprised if you had reacted

differently. You must remember you haven't held her since the day she was born. You couldn't have expected it to be otherwise."

* * *

"It really was terrible, wasn't it? Tell me it wasn't just me," said Jenny.

"Yes, it was terrible. Bloody awful is a better way of putting it, I think," replied John as he poured himself another cup of coffee.

"What did you make of her?"

"I'm not sure. I felt towards the end there might have been something of a breakthrough. I thought the way Laura reacted to her might have had some effect, but that woman intervened when I mentioned the court case."

"I suppose there's more chance now, though, that she might change her mind. She's seen Laura and knows she's well. She has seen us and knows we are normal and has also seen how close Laura is to us. Surely that must have some effect on her."

"It must, I suppose. Whatever happens, I'm sure this meeting has done us no harm in so far as the court case is concerned. We've been more than reasonable in co-operating with Laura's biological mother and Laura's reaction to her must be of some help to us."

"She looked so hurt when Laura wouldn't go to her. It must be dreadful to be rejected by your own child like that."

"I suppose it must," John replied wearily, getting up from the table and carrying some of the dirty dishes over to the sink. "I just hope she understands now that she's no longer Laura's mother but simply a stranger."

"I hope if we all end up in court, the judge will understand that too," Jenny sighed.

* * *

The nose. She could not take her mind off the nose and she could not understand why. It made her feel so angry. The miracle of again seeing Laura seemed overshadowed by the nose. She tried to remember what Laura looked like. The image of a tiny baby had now been replaced by that of a little girl with an oversized pug nose. I must stop this, Colette said to herself as she again turned on the hot-water tap to heat up the bath she had been sitting in for over an hour.

A more normal picture of Laura replaced the nose in her thoughts.

"She really is so beautiful, so beautiful. How could I have given away anything so beautiful?" she said to an empty bathroom.

Away from the influence of St Mark's and the adopters, Colette knew that Laura was her child and she no longer had any doubts. She definitely wanted her back and was determined to win her court case.

sixteen

"The fact that the mother agreed to Laura being placed with the adopters so soon after her birth could be a problem for us in court. There is the possibility that the court could take the view that she wasn't given sufficient time to consider her situation, that her agreement was not voluntary, that she was in some way pressurised. If that view were taken, the court could not permit the Adoption Authority to dispense with the need for the mother's final consent and it could not authorise the Authority to make an adoption order. I am not saying that will happen; I just want to warn you that it is possible."

John and Jenny were sitting in Galloway's office. It was two weeks away from the court hearing and they were having what Galloway referred to as a "pre-hearing consultation".

"If that were to happen, could Laura be taken from us and returned to her?" John asked apprehensively.

"That would then become a real possibility," Galloway replied. "Laura has been with you both for just fourteen months. If adoption is ruled out, due to the court holding the mother's placement agreement to be invalid, the court might very well go on to hold that in such circumstances it is in the interest of Laura's welfare that she be brought up by her mother. Alternatively, the court could make a custody order in your favour and just give the mother visitation rights. What would happen in such circumstances could depend ultimately on the personality of the judge who hears the case and what importance he attaches to the mother's constitutional rights."

"What you are saying is that, even if we are not allowed to adopt Laura, the court might not automatically take her away from us and return her to the mother," said John, trying to calm Jenny's nerves.

"You mean, in that case Laura could be left in our custody but we might have to keep meeting the mother with Laura at St Mark's?" Jenny asked.

"The court initially could allow the mother to visit Laura every two to three weeks or so in your home and then, as Laura gets older, her visitation rights could increase and she could be allowed to take Laura out with her. Eventually, the court might allow Laura to stay with her biological mother for holiday periods."

"What would happen if Laura got to like her? Could the positions change? Could she be given custody at some later stage?" Jenny was apprehensive.

"That's a possibility," Galloway replied. "I'm sorry

but I have to explain to you that on the basis of what we now know there can be no certainty about the outcome. My job is to do everything I can to secure the court orders that you require to adopt Laura. I must also explain the problems and prepare you for the possibility that the court could require you to return Laura to her mother."

"What if the court is satisfied that she did voluntarily agree to place Laura for adoption?" It was John who put the question. "Do we automatically succeed then?"

"If that happens, you are in a much stronger position. The mother's constitutional rights cease to be relevant, the possibility of adoption is opened up and the only thing the court need consider then is Laura's best interests. On that issue, Dr O'Connell's report is very definite. She says that Laura has fully bonded with you and she strongly favours adoption. However, the mother's psychiatrist, Dr Lloyd, while acknowledging that bonding has taken place, states that in his view the mother could properly care for Laura. Whilst he admits that Laura may suffer some initial stress from being moved, he expresses the opinion that if she is brought up by the mother in her family home with the support of the grandparents, Laura will form new attachments and bonds to replace existing ones. While he makes no final recommendation his report is more favourably disposed to the mother. However, the fact that Laura has been with you for almost fourteen months and that both psychiatrists agree that she has formed bonds will, I hope, tip the balance in our favour, if we overcome the placement problem. The way in which the psychiatrists' evidence comes across in court will also be important. It is a great pity that the mother didn't wait just another few months before going to court. Your position would have been much stronger if she had done so."

"So at this stage you cannot predict the outcome for us?" John said.

"All I can say is that I will do everything possible to bring about a successful result," Galloway answered, trying to give them some reassurance. "The job I have to do would have been a lot easier and your case would have been a good deal stronger if the mother had waited until Laura was five or six weeks old before she agreed to her placement with you and if she had waited another three or four months before bringing court proceedings."

* * *

"Galloway's whole attitude worries me. He is always so cautious, so unwilling to commit himself. You would think with his reputation and experience that he would know by now what is likely to happen in court. He seems to hedge all the time."

"I suppose it's understandable," Ruth replied as she handed a cup of lemon tea to Jenny. "He's on your side, he wants you to win, but presumably if the outcome was a foregone conclusion the lawyers would be advising the mother against a contest. They would be telling her she would lose and that there would be no point in it. If the law was so simple and certain there would never be any court cases. I'd be concerned if Galloway wasn't being a little careful about making predictions."

Ruth and David had invited John and Jenny over for spaghetti bolognese and had talked them into leaving Laura with a baby-sitter for the first time in weeks. The meal was over and they were sitting around a log fire in the lounge, drinking tea and eating pieces of a lemon sponge cake that Ruth had baked that day.

"I just wish it was all over. It's like living a nightmare. I sometimes pinch myself in the hope that I'll wake up and discover that it is all unreal, that the adoption order has been made and none of this is happening," said Jenny.

"But it will be over in a few weeks and everything will return to normal. *Then* you'll have another problem – deciding who to invite to the celebration." Ruth was determined to be cheerful.

"But what if we should lose?"

"Don't even think like that, Jenny," David intervened. "Be positive. Don't keep on filling yourself with doubts and worries. Everything is going well so far and there is no reason why it should not all turn out well in the end. Laura has been with you both for over a year and I'm convinced you will win in court."

Jenny was not so sure, She couldn't stop worrying and she had difficulty eating and sleeping. As the court hearing crept nearer, she became more and more anxious. The thought of going into the courtroom and giving evidence in the witness box terrified her. What would happen if she was a bad witness, or if she could not understand the questions she was asked, or if she gave the wrong answers or if the judge did not like her? What would they do if Paul Galloway became ill and could not appear in court? What would the judge's decision be if Miss Hennessy accused them of baby-battering or if the mother's evidence aroused everyone's sympathy?

"Why don't we just leave Ireland and take Laura with us?" she asked John in bed five nights before the court hearing.

"Should we go now or tomorrow morning?"

"I'm serious. If we were simply to leave and take Laura with us, what could anyone do?"

"How would we live? What would happen to my company, to this house? What would happen if we were caught and imprisoned for kidnapping? We've got to face it, Jenny. We've lived with this for five months and in another few days it will be all over. We have to be brave and face up to it."

Jenny cuddled into his shoulder and started to sob. Her whole body was shaking and he felt her tears wet on his neck. He had a tightening in his own chest and wanted to cry with her, but told himself not to, that he must not. It was good she was getting some of the pent-up emotion out of her system, but he had to appear strong and confident; otherwise she might collapse totally and be unable to go to court. He had to be brave for both of them and for Laura.

seventeen

Colette sat in Robert Barnes' office and listened attentively to him.

"The reports from the two child psychiatrists both say that Laura has bonded with the adopters, regards them as her parents and will suffer a great deal of stress if removed from them. Dr O'Connell recommends that Laura remain with the adopters. Dr Lloyd states that if Laura is returned to you she will eventually develop new bonds and attachments. His report is a good deal more favourable, but he does not expressly recommend that Laura be returned to you."

Colette had talked to both psychiatrists, found them both sympathetic and understanding and had assumed that their reports would be helpful to her case.

"Of course Laura is attached to the adopters!" she retorted. "She hardly knows me. She has been brought up by them but she is *my* child, *my* daughter. We played together with a biscuit in St Mark's. She would not have played with me like that if she had not known that I was her real mother."

"The reports say that she does not have any instinctive relationship with you and that, although you are her biological mother, she has no recognition of this at present."

"I don't believe that. I don't and won't accept that!" Colette was shouting now, her composure disintegrating.

"I'm only telling you this so that you will understand the difficulties we have to surmount if you are to succeed." Robert Barnes was speaking gently and soothingly. "The trial judge will hear all of this in evidence and will be considerably influenced by it. The evidence of your social worker, Mrs Comerford, will, I believe, be helpful to us. In her report she describes you as a 'sensitive person who suffered considerable personal trauma at the time of Laura's birth and immediately subsequent to it'. We are going to have to try and convince the judge that you were so distressed and traumatised when Laura was born that you were unable to make a valid agreement to her being placed with adopters – in essence, that you were unable to think clearly and make rational decisions."

"Does that mean that you are going to suggest that I went mad or crazy or something?"

"No. Simply that you were so upset you were not thinking clearly enough to make clear decisions about Laura's future. If the court accepts that, we can prevent an adoption order being made and greatly increase the possibility of Laura being returned to you. However, it is important for you to know that even if we succeed in preventing an adoption order from being made, the court could still permit Laura to remain with the adopters and make a custody order in their favour. If that happened, you would be given visitation rights to her. While it would be unusual for the court to decide your case in that way, it is possible and cannot be ruled out."

"You mean if we prevent an adoption order being made, I won't get Laura back automatically?" Colette was incredulous.

"I'm saying that the court could decide that for the time being Laura should remain in the adopters' care. Such a decision would not be permanent. As she got older and you build up a relationship with her, you could then seek custody again. I am not saying this will happen. It is just one of the possibilities. If everything goes our way, Laura will be returned to you. I just cannot be sure of the outcome. If this case had been heard when Laura was only five or six months old, you would have been in a much stronger position. It is important that you understand that it is going to be an uphill battle."

The implications of what Colette's solicitor was saying to her slowly sank in. Why had she not told Michael O'Brien earlier and sought his help? If only she had done so it would have been so much easier to get Laura back.

"Maybe the psychiatrists are wrong. Maybe the judge will not accept what they say. I don't believe Laura could be so attached to strangers." Her voice trailed off as she fought her emotions.

"It's my job to try and prove them wrong and I will do my very best for you," replied Barnes soothingly.

* * *

"They're all wrong! I know that if Laura is returned to me, she will quickly realise I am her mother, her real mother, not an adoptive mother. She'll soon settle down."

Michael O'Brien had joined Colette for lunch at the self-service restaurant in Leinster House, but she had only picked at the food that she had selected at the counter. They were now talking over coffee.

"It doesn't seem to be as simple as that," he replied, anxious not to upset her but also trying to ensure that she did not build up her expectations to unrealistic levels. "I think you've got to prepare yourself for the possibility that Laura may not be returned to you."

"Even you think it's hopeless now, that I'm wasting my time."

"No, I am not saying that. If you want to try to get Laura back, you have no choice but to go to court, but I think you've got to be prepared for the possibility that you might lose."

Colette was not prepared to accept that possibility. She couldn't come to terms with the idea that if

Laura's adoption was given the go-ahead by the court, she would be prevented from seeing Laura for the rest of her life. They had been part of each other's lives for the nine months of her pregnancy. Laura was her daughter and she was her only real mother but everyone seemed to forget that. No one attached any importance to that fact.

The court hearing was four days away. The adopters' evidence was to be presented on the first day, a Monday, Colette's evidence on the following day. Colette was not allowed to be present in the court on the Monday and the adopters, she was told, would not be there on the Tuesday. They were excluded from hearing each other's evidence so that their true identity would not be revealed. Colette resented the secrecy. She wanted to know the real names of the good-looking couple whom she had met in St Mark's, what the husband worked at, whether they had any other children, whether they were poor or rich, where they lived, where Laura lived. Now she had become suspicious that Barnes was no longer on her side and had a feeling that he was only pretending to help her because of his friendship with Michael O'Brien, not because he believed that Laura should be returned to her.

How could she rely on him to ensure that she was properly represented in court, not only on the day she was to be present but more particularly on the Monday when she was prevented from being there? How could she be certain that he was not now on the adopters' side? Laura's future life was being fought over and decided in that courtroom. Colette could not understand a law that refused her, Laura's mother, admission to the courtroom on the day the adopters were to give evidence. Was something being hidden from her? Was there something about these adopters that everyone believed should be concealed? She had no objection to the adopters being present to hear her evidence. Why then should she be excluded from hearing theirs?

As the day of the court hearing drew nearer, Colette's suspicions and distrust grew. She went through the motions of accepting Robert Barnes' advice and arranged with her parents and Sally Thomas that they would all go to the court together on the Tuesday. The three of them in addition to Colette, Mrs Comerford and the child psychiatrist, Dr Lloyd, were to give evidence on that day. By now, Colette had almost completely abandoned any hope that she would win in court, that she would succeed in having Laura returned to her or prevent an adoption order from being made. Everyone, she had decided, was now on the side of the adopters. Maybe not her parents or Sally, but certainly everyone who mattered. The whole court process was biased against her and designed to stop her from winning, even up to the point of preventing her from hearing things said in court that could be in her favour and stopping her making sure that her lawyers did their job properly.

Colette no longer expected to win in court. But

she was going to make use of the fact that the adopters had come to court, to put together a plan of her own to get Laura back. If she could not depend on others, she could still depend on herself. This was her last opportunity and she had to take it. She would show them all.

eighteen

It was almost the end of March and freezing cold. A thick frost had painted the grass white overnight and dark grey clouds threatened snow but John and Jenny were oblivious to the weather conditions as they entered the unfamiliar court building. The court hearing was to begin at eleven o'clock. Paul Galloway had told them to meet him at nine forty-five in Ó'Dálaigh House, a four-storey redbrick building beside the Four Courts on Inns Quay that fronted onto the River Liffey. They had arrived exactly on time, accompanied by Jenny's parents, and took the lift to the fourth floor where the special Family High Court sat. As Galloway had directed, they took over an empty consultation room and awaited his arrival. He came twenty minutes late, just as they were starting to wonder whether he had forgotten all about them. When they were all sitting around a table in the consulting room, he tried to reassure them.

"We should start right on eleven o'clock. There's no other case in the court list ahead of us. I'll start by giving the judge a brief introduction to the evidence we are presenting and then I'll call you first, Jenny, to give evidence and after you it will be John's turn. I'll then call Jenny's parents, Mr and Mrs Edmonds, Mrs Gavin and Dr O'Connell in that order. Mrs Gavin will be here in a few minutes; Dr O'Connell will be arriving at about eleven. When I'm finished the Adoption Authority will put Miss Hennessy into the witness box and that will be all until tomorrow."

Jenny was only half-listening. It all seemed unreal. She felt caught up in a story – someone else's story – and could not believe that it was all really happening to her. She and John had tried so hard to have a child of their own, taken so long to make the decision to adopt and felt so elated when Laura was placed with them. Neither she nor John had ever thought their being able to adopt could all depend on winning a courtroom battle. Mrs Gavin had remarked to them that if it all went wrong and if they lost, St Mark's could find them another baby to adopt as soon as possible, but she and John had agreed that they didn't want to adopt another baby. What they wanted was to adopt Laura.

Jenny kept telling herself what Paul Galloway had said: that even if the court prevented them from adopting Laura, she might not be taken from them. But Jenny no longer believed this. She thought he was just trying to keep up her morale for the court hearing.

"Is there anything any of you wants to ask me?" Galloway's question interrupted her thoughts.

"I don't think so," replied John.

"Just one thing," said Jenny. "Is there no way we can come down here tomorrow and hear the mother's evidence? It's so cruel to be prevented from being in court and seeing what's going on when Laura's whole future depends on it."

"I'm afraid it's not possible," replied Galloway. "The mother is in the same position. She is prevented from being here today. You're going to have to rely on me to do my job properly and to report back to you on what takes place in court tomorrow. As soon as tomorrow's hearing is over, I'll phone you and tell you how everything is going," he promised.

Fifteen minutes later John and Jenny were sitting in the courtroom listening to Galloway giving the judge a brief outline of the case. Mrs Gavin had arrived but had to remain in the waiting room with Jenny's parents until she was called to give evidence. The courtroom was small and informal and was quite different to what either of them had envisaged. It bore no resemblance to the intimidating courtrooms they had become accustomed to seeing on the television and at the movies. The judge, a man called Flannery was seated on a chair on a raised platform behind a big modern desk made of lightly grained wood. Directly below him in the well of the court sat the registrar and a court note-taker. A few feet away beside them was positioned the slightly elevated witness box.

Galloway was standing behind a large table, in front of and parallel to the judge's desk. On Galloway's right were seated a solicitor and two barristers representing the Adoption Authority and next to them a solicitor and two barristers representing the mother.

The barristers all looked very formidable. Besides them Paul Galloway looked small and insignificant. On Galloway's left sat Ciaran Griffin, Galloway's young assistant, whom John and Jenny had met in his office and whose job it was to take notes and bring their witnesses from the consultation room into the courtroom when they were called to give evidence by Galloway.

John had known that the mother would be represented by a barrister but had not expected two. He wondered whether he had made a mistake in not insisting that Galloway instruct barristers to appear in court on their behalf. Their solicitor looked such a slight figure standing there, when compared with the tall, important-looking barristers acting as advocates for the mother and the Adoption Authority.

"And now I call Jennifer Masterson to give evidence," announced Galloway, concluding his opening comments.

Jenny stood up and walked over to the witness box.

Before she could sit down, she was handed a Bible by the registrar. "Repeat after me, please: I swear by Almighty God . . ."

"I swear by Almighty God," Jenny hesitantly repeated.

"To tell the truth and nothing but the truth."

She again repeated the registrar's words and then returned to him the Bible that she had been handed.

"Please sit down," the judge said to Jenny, gesturing towards the chair behind her.

She felt her heart thumping and a peculiar sensation in her legs.

Galloway asked her the same questions he had put to her in his office two weeks earlier and Jenny gave the same answers. It was surprisingly easy and she quickly settled down. She detailed their marital history, the medical help they had sought to have a child of their own, their decision to adopt, Laura's progress since being placed with them and Laura's reaction to her biological mother at the meeting that had taken place in St Mark's. Galloway encouraged her to speak about Laura's relationship with Jenny's sister and brother-in-law and with her parents and even Rebel the dog got a special mention.

"Why have you not complied with the mother's request to return Laura to her?" was Galloway's final question.

"Because we love her and she loves us. Because she is our child and we are her parents. I believe she would be devastated if we gave her back to a mother whom she doesn't know and if she were to lose contact not only with us but also with all our family, friends and relations whom she knows so well."

Galloway sat down and Jenny stood up to leave the witness box, pleased with herself that it was all over and delighted with her last reply. This she had rehearsed over and over again, knowing what Galloway's final question to her was going to be.

Judge Flannery said, "Just a moment, Mrs Masterson. The mother's counsel may wish to ask you some questions. Have you any questions you wish to put to the witness, Mrs Dell?"

A tall woman, peering through a pair of thick glasses, stood up, her long auburn hair sticking out the sides and back of her wig. At the beginning of the case she had been identified to the judge as Elizabeth Dell, the senior counsel instructed to act for Colette James.

"Just a few brief questions, judge," she answered, looking straight at Jenny. "You say Laura has developed very well and there have been no particular problems?"

"Yes, that's correct."

"And there has been no disruption in the progress she has made?"

"No," replied Jenny, wondering what the counsel was getting at.

"So she was not in any way distressed as a result of meeting her mother in St Mark's?"

"No, I did not say that," replied Jenny uncomfortably. "What I said earlier was that she became upset when sitting on the mother's lap and, when the mother asked to hold her a second time, she clung to me and started to cry."

"But this didn't affect her in any way when the visit was over?"

"No, that's true," Jenny confirmed lamely.

Mrs Dell sat down and the Adoption Authority's barristers remained seated, indicating that there were no questions that they wished to ask.

"Thank you very much, Mrs Masterson. You may step down now," the judge said, smiling at her.

"I now call John Masterson," said Paul Galloway.

John stood up, entered the witness box, took the oath and repeated much of the same evidence already given by Jenny.

The day wore on. Jenny's parents said what good parents their daughter and son-in-law were and how attached everyone was to Laura. Mrs Gavin confirmed that Laura had settled in well and that the Mastersons were "a fine couple". Dr O'Connell, in reply to Galloway's questions, said that Laura had bonded well, was used to her surroundings and would, in her own view, be permanently scarred psychologically if she were to be removed from the Mastersons.

Mrs Dell then stood up to cross-examine Dr O'Connell.

"In your evidence you are very definite that Laura should remain with the adopters. Is that not correct?"

"That is my view."

"You set no store by the fact that Laura's biological mother is her own flesh and blood?"

"Laura has no relationship with the biological mother. She does not know her to be her mother."

"The biological mother gave birth to the child, did she not, doctor?"

"She did."

"Is it possible that there might be some instinctual relationship between Laura and her biological mother?"

"I'm sure there is at present no such relationship. All the modern work in this area emphasises the importance of psychological parent over the biological parent," answered Dr O'Connell.

"Doctor, is it not correct that for many years emphasis was laid on the importance of the biological or blood link between parent and child and that it was generally accepted by child psychiatrists that a child was better off with its biological parents or parent? Is that not correct?"

"Well, there was always some controversy about that. I suppose you are right, however, in what you say."

"Why is there now a change of approach, doctor?"

"All recent research and modern psychiatric thinking emphasises the importance of the psychological parent of the child – that is, the person that the child identifies with the carrying-on of parental functions."

"If those functions were transferred from the adopters to the mother, would the child not start to identify with the mother?"

"She would after some time, but the stress caused to her by being removed from the adopters and from everything she is familiar with would have a devastating impact on her development."

"'Could' or 'would', Dr O'Connell?" Mrs Dell asked sharply.

"I believe it would."

"Doctor, is that belief based on your own experience in working with children who have been so affected, or on research results?"

"Largely on research. I haven't worked with any children who have been returned to their biological parents in such circumstances."

"So your belief is not based on your own experience?"

"It is based on my knowledge and training and fifteen years' experience as a senior child psychiatrist," Dr O'Connell replied, becoming increasingly irritated by the probing questions being asked of her.

"Doctor, it was fashionable until relatively recently to believe in the blood link – the idea that there was some sort of mystical or instinctual relationship between mother and child that survived even an immediate separation following the child's birth. Is that not right?"

"It was fashionable until about forty years ago."

"It is fashionable today to emphasise psychological parenting. Might it not be the case, doctor, that in thirty years' time this theory in turn may no longer be tenable?" asked Mrs Dell.

"I cannot look into a crystal ball and answer that," Dr O'Connell snapped.

Mrs Dell sat down, her cross-examination concluded. She felt satisfied that to some extent she had undermined Dr O'Connell's evidence. There were other questions she would have liked to ask but she was uncertain what answers might have resulted and she was concerned that she might harm Colette James' case if she pushed matters further.

Paul Galloway slowly stood up. He felt that before Dr O'Connell left the witness box, he should re-establish in the judge's mind the essential nature of her evidence.

"Dr O'Connell, bearing in mind the assessment you have carried out of the parties involved in this case, what course of action do you believe is in the best interests of the child Laura?"

"I believe that she should remain with the adopters," Dr O'Connell responded without hesitation.

"That belief, doctor, is based on your assessment of what might occur if she were removed from the adopters, is that not so?" asked Judge Flannery, intervening for the first time.

"That is right, I suppose," replied Dr O'Connell, uncertain of where the judge was leading.

"In other words you are predicting that Laura would suffer both short-term and long-term developmental problems if she were to be removed from the adopters."

"Yes, that's right."

"Is that not also crystal-ball-gazing, doctor?" asked the judge.

Dr O'Connell hesitated. She knew in her heart that Laura should remain with the Mastersons, and now felt trapped by her earlier over-hasty answer to Mrs Dell. No sound could be heard in the courtroom as everyone awaited her response.

"No, judge," she replied. "My view and my recommendation that Laura should remain with the adopters is a result of my seeing her interacting with them and other members of her family. The child clearly not only regards the adopters as her father and mother but is also very close to many others in the extended family. If this child is removed from this family setting and cut off from all of those with whom she has established relationships and from everything with which she is familiar, she will suffer very greatly. All my working experience leads me to the conclusion that in her later life Laura would, as a result, suffer serious psychiatric illness and have great difficulty in maintaining stable relationships as an adult."

Galloway had no more questions. He breathed a sigh of relief, feeling that Dr O'Connell's last reply had undone much of the damage that had been caused by Mrs Dell's careful and clever cross-examination.

"Dr O'Connell was my final witness and that completes my evidence, judge," he concluded, slowly sinking onto his chair. He knew that for him the easiest part of the case had been completed. There could be no doubt in anybody's mind that the Mastersons were fine people and the evidence heard so far had established in the judge's mind their obvious love for Laura and her very strong attachment to them. Jenny's parents had been presented as the perfect grandparents and Dr O'Connell had testified that Laura's welfare required that she remain in her adoptive home. Yet Judge Flannery's attitude to Dr O'Connell's evidence was unsettling. Mrs Dell had clearly been successful in raising some doubts in the judge's mind about the importance to be attached to the concept of psychological parenting.

As Dr O'Connell stepped out of the witness box, Robert Barnes felt that some progress had been made in discrediting the mass of psychiatric evidence that supported his opponents' case. If only, he thought, Dr O'Connell had not so competently replied to the judge's final question.

It was now the turn of the Adoption Authority. Imelda Hennessy walked into the witness box, a large bandage visible around her right leg, below the knee.

"How many times did you visit the adopters' home?" Adrian Owen, one of the Adoption Authority's barristers, asked.

"On six occasions."

"What conclusions did you draw?"

"Well, the baby settled in well, but I had my doubts."

"Can you explain your last comment?"

"Everything seemed to go too well. The adopters never expressed any worries or concerns to me. Everything doesn't normally go so smoothly."

"Had you any reason for this view?"

"It's something that's difficult to put your finger on. The first time I called, Mrs Masterson seemed surprised or put out by my arrival. The baby had a large bruise on her forehead which was referred to in the report of the adoption society's social worker that I received a day or so before my visit. I asked how it had occurred and Mrs Masterson seemed evasive and nervous when replying."

"Did you draw any conclusions from this?"

"I had my suspicions."

"What did you suspect?"

"That they might not be caring for the child properly."

"Did you ever find the child bruised on any other occasion?"

"No, but there were other matters that I was anxious about. For example, the dog never left the child alone. It was forever licking it."

"Why do you object to that?"

"It's unhealthy. Dogs are dirty and dangerous animals. They should never be let near babies; you never know what might happen."

"Were all the visits you made by way of carrying out an assessment?"

"Five of them were. On the sixth occasion I called to tell the Mastersons that the mother had started this court case."

"What was their reaction on that occasion?"

"They didn't have any reaction. I was astonished. I thought they would be upset but it didn't seem to affect them at all. They didn't even offer me a cup of tea, just showed me to the door a few minutes after I arrived."

"What is your view of the Mastersons?"

"I haven't yet finished my assessment, but I would say that they are a very unfriendly couple."

"What, in your view, should happen to the child?"

"I don't think I can answer that until I have finished my assessment."

Adrian Owen sat down and it was Paul Galloway's turn to cross-examine.

John and Jenny could not take their eyes off Imelda Hennessy. They had found her a difficult woman to get on with but had always been courteous to her. They had presumed that the views she expressed would be similar to these of Mrs Gavin and they felt that her unexpected hostility to them was totally unfair. Jenny wanted to shout out that she was a liar, to tell the judge not to believe her, but knew she must stay silent. The Mastersons watched Galloway stand up.

"Miss Hennessy. What are your qualifications?" he asked.

"I beg your pardon?"

"Your qualifications as an Adoption Authority social worker. What training did you undertake to qualify as a social worker?"

"I have worked with the Adoption Authority and its predecessor the Adoption Board for over thirty years," she replied.

"Do you have any degree or professional qualifications in social work or social sciences?"

"Yes, I have a post-graduate degree in social work and social science."

"What did you mean when you said the child settled down too well?"

"Well, usually there are a few teething problems,

such as the adopters coping with feeding or nappy-changing or baby not sleeping well, or nappy rash."

"And you say there were no such problems?"

"I was told none."

"And that made you suspicious. Suspicious of what?"

"Suspicious that the adopters were not being frank with me."

"Couldn't it simply have been that none of these problems occurred?"

"Well, I suppose so."

"You referred to bruising on the child and the report of the adoption society social worker," Galloway said.

"Yes, that's right."

"Did you ask for any explanation as to how the bruising had occurred?"

"Yes."

"And what was the explanation you were given?"

"I was told the baby had been playing on the floor and had bumped her forehead into the coffee table." The witness was obviously uncomfortable.

"Have you any reason to disbelieve that explanation?" Galloway asked.

"Mrs Masterson seemed very nervous when I asked about it."

"Have you any reason to disbelieve her explanation?" Galloway repeated abruptly.

"Well . . . no . . . not really."

"When Mrs Gavin was giving evidence, she said

that both the Mastersons were very upset when they learned that the mother wanted Laura back. But you say that they did not appear upset when you told them about the court proceedings?"

"Yes, that's right."

"Could it not be possible they may not have wished to reveal their feelings to you?"

"I suppose that is possible," Imelda Hennessy replied uncertainly.

Paul Galloway sat down and Mrs Dell rose.

"Miss Hennessy, do you believe that Laura should remain with the adopters or not?"

"If you are asking me if she should be returned to her mother, I can't answer that; I haven't met the mother. But if you're asking me if an adoption order should be made, I would have to say that I haven't yet finished my assessment."

"But you have doubts about the adoption?"

"I am not yet satisfied about everything, but I don't think I can say any more than that."

Mrs Dell sat down and the judge gestured to Imelda Hennessy that she could leave the witness box.

Galloway watched her climb down the step and limp towards her seat. Remembering something he had overheard earlier, he suddenly had an idea.

"Sorry, judge, there is just one question I should have asked the witness," he said, jumping to his feet.

"Very well, Mr Galloway," the judge replied with a look of slight irritation. "Could you just return to the witness box for a moment, Miss Hennessy, please?"

Imelda Hennessy turned and with evident discomfort climbed back into the witness box and sat down.

"Just one small matter, Miss Hennessy," said Galloway. "What is wrong with your leg?"

Before the witness could reply, Adrian Owen was on his feet.

"Really, judge, I can't see what relevance that question has to this case. I must object," he protested.

"Well, Mr Galloway, you didn't bring the witness back to answer that question, did you? Surely that is not relevant?" queried the judge, sighing.

"I'm sorry, judge," Paul Galloway replied. "I'm afraid it might be. If your lordship could just bear with me?"

"Very well, proceed. We shall see," the judge responded.

"Your leg, Miss Hennessy – what is wrong exactly?"

"A dog. I was bitten by a fox terrier that belongs to my next-door neighbour. I have got my solicitor on to it."

"I take it then you do not like dogs?" Galloway suggested.

"I certainly do not," she replied, bewilderment as to why she had been asked such a question clearly etched on her face.

"Thank you, that is all, judge," Galloway concluded, sitting down.

As Imelda Hennessy struggled out of the witness box for the second time that day, Paul Galloway felt pleased with himself. He thought that his cross-examination had raised doubts in the judge's mind as to the credibility of the curiously hostile and unhelpful evidence given by the cantankerous social worker. Now Rebel's reputation had been salvaged from critical assessment. As far as dogs and the dangers they posed for children were concerned, not even Mr Justice Flannery could regard Imelda Hennessy's evidence as being that of a neutral and unbiased witness.

* * *

Mentally and physically drained after their day in court, John and Jenny Masterson did not notice the yellow Ford Fiesta that followed them home. They hadn't seen it pull out behind them as they drove off from Ó'Dálaigh House or registered the blaring of horns when it raced through red traffic lights in Terenure after John had crossed the junction on the amber light. They did not even notice it slow down as their car turned into the long driveway to their home.

Colette James felt pleased with herself. She now knew where they lived and, more important, where Laura lived. It had been a long day. She had watched them walk into the court building early that morning and had waited in her car for them to leave. She recognised the psychiatrist whom she had seen at the Mastersons' request and the woman from the adoption society who had been present at the meeting in St

Mark's. At around one o'clock she watched them all come out and go into a pub next door to the court.

Colette had met her own barristers only the previous Friday in preparation for the court hearing, but they were easily recognisable, hurrying down the steps a few minutes later accompanied by Robert Barnes and walking off in the direction of the Four Courts. She knew that that was where most of the High Court cases in Dublin were heard, Ó'Dálaigh House being used only for the determination of family disputes. She had driven up the quays and allowed herself twenty minutes to nibble at a sandwich and drink a cup of coffee in O'Leary's Bar before driving back to Ó'Dálaigh House in good time to park her car and see them all going in again.

The afternoon dragged on. She sat in her car watching two men in 'Dublin Street Parking Services' day-glo jackets clamping cars along the quays. On one occasion a tramp passing by had looked questioningly into Colette's car but quickly moved on when she stared back at him.

It had been a long and wearisome day but it had proved worthwhile. The address of the house in which the adopters were keeping Laura from Colette was no longer a mystery.

nineteen

Colette was sitting in a chair at the back of the courtroom as Mrs Dell concluded her opening description of the evidence she would present to the court. Colette's parents, Sally Thomas, Dr Lloyd, Mrs Comerford and Michael O'Brien were all sitting in a large waiting room next door to the court. Robert Barnes had telephoned Michael O'Brien the previous evening and a decision had been made to call him as a witness. Although Michael had not known about Laura until Colette had told him her story about ten months after Laura's birth, Barnes thought that his evidence of her behaviour throughout the time he had known her could help to establish Colette's general state of mind and confirm the account that would be given by Sally Thomas. Michael O'Brien, who was anxious to give whatever help he could, readily agreed to make himself available.

"In essence, my case is that at the time Colette

James agreed to place her baby for adoption, she was so distressed, confused and frightened that she did not freely and voluntarily agree to give up her child: that accordingly her placement agreement was and remains invalid and no order should or can be made by this court to enable the adoption process to be completed – that Colette James should not be permanently deprived of her daughter as the adopters contend but that this court should order that her daughter be returned to her sole custody."

Mrs Dell concluded her opening statement by calling Colette to give evidence.

Colette stood up and walked slowly up to the witness box. She repeated the oath as it was read out to her by the court registrar. He sat down and she remained standing.

"Please, sit down, Miss James," Judge Flannery said, gesturing in the direction of the seat behind her.

Colette sat down and quietly and firmly answered the questions put to her as Mrs Dell took her through the formal part of her evidence. Her name, her date of birth, her address, the names of her parents, her educational qualifications, her employment since completing her education and the date of Laura's birth were all recited for the court record.

"Before leaving school, did you have any boyfriends?" Mrs Dell asked.

"A few . . . I went out with a few different boys but there was no one special, no one that I was particularly attached to."

"Before leaving school, did you at any time engage in sexual intercourse?"

"No, of course not."

"When did you first have sexual intercourse?"

"About a year before Laura was born."

"Laura – that's the name of your child?"

"Yes, that's right."

"With whom did you first have sexual intercourse?"

"With Laura's father," Colette replied awkwardly.

"Have you ever had intercourse with anyone other than Laura's father?"

"No," Colette replied emphatically.

"Who is Laura's father?"

Colette had not expected that question and she hesitated. She had never discussed with her barrister, Mrs Dell, the arrangement that Michael O'Brien had made with Brannigan but Robert Barnes was aware of it and she presumed that he had told Mrs Dell. Although she was now reconciled with her parents, she had still not told them that Brannigan was Laura's father and she had no wish to reopen old wounds which would inevitably lead to a serious showdown between Brannigan and her own father.

"Sorry, what did you ask me?" she asked, buying time.

"The father, what is his name?"

"I don't want to say unless I really have to."

"She is your client, Mrs Dell, but if she does not wish to state the father's name, it is not essential that she should do so," intervened Judge Flannery.

"Is he a public figure?"

"Yes," Colette replied cautiously.

"Do you still have a relationship with him?"

"No, I do not."

"Is there any possibility you might marry Laura's father at some time in the future?"

"Absolutely not."

"When did your relationship end?"

"After I told him I was pregnant." Colette was presuming that Mrs Dell's question did not refer to her working relationship with Brannigan.

The questioning continued and Colette described her actions in the months leading up to Laura's birth, explaining why she had concealed the pregnancy from her parents.

"When you told the father that you were pregnant, did he give you any advice?" asked Mrs Dell.

"He suggested I should have an abortion," came the reply.

"Did you consider that to be an option?"

"No. I couldn't. I wouldn't . . . it was not something I would ever do."

"Did he offer you any other help?"

"No. Well, not at that time."

"Were you upset by his reaction?"

"I think I was shocked by the whole thing. I never expected to become pregnant. He had always assured me that he was taking precautions. It was not something I had ever thought about. I suppose I was in shock when I told him about it."

"Why did you place Laura for adoption?"

"I thought there was no alternative. I believed my parents would never talk to me again if they knew and I was also terrified as to how my father would react if he discovered the father's identity. It seemed to me at that time to be the only available option. I felt I had no choice."

Mrs Dell continued to ask the questions that would create in the judge's mind a picture of Colette as a scared young girl thrown into shock and confusion by her pregnancy and by the shattering reaction of the father of her child. Colette described moving into the flat with her friend Sally and gave her reasons for doing so. She responded to questions about the meeting she had had with Mrs Comerford before Laura's birth and then about her stay in hospital.

"Why did you refuse to see Laura after the day she was born?"

"Because I was terrified that if I saw her, I would change my mind, that I would want to keep her, and I knew that was impossible."

"Did you want to see her?"

"Of course I did but I kept on telling myself that I mustn't give in to my feelings. I tried to shut her out of my mind."

"In what way?"

"By playing a game – playing a trick in a way. I told myself that I was in hospital because I was sick and that I would be going home in a few days. I pretended that any arrangements I had to make about Laura were on behalf of some other unmarried mother and did not relate to me personally. By the time I left hospital, I had convinced myself I had been ill, not pregnant."

"Did anyone suggest to you that you should see Laura again before she went to adopters?"

"Yes, various nurses who did not understand my situation and Mrs Comerford, my social worker from St Mark's."

"And you always refused to see her again?"

"Yes."

Colette gave the court an outline of her lifestyle after she had left hospital. Mrs Dell questioned her about the evening she had visited the home of Michael O'Brien's sister.

"Why did you take ill that night?"

"It was the baby . . . its crying, her feeding it. Everything suddenly came crashing in on me. I realised that I had been pretending to myself for all those months that I had never been pregnant, that I had no baby. The enormity of what I had done suddenly hit me . . . I can't explain it any better than that."

Colette was fighting a losing battle to retain her composure. It was the first time she'd had to explain fully to anyone the reason for her collapse on that night. She now understood that the sight of that baby had jolted her back to reality and that she had been overcome by a terrible feeling of loss. It was as if someone she loved dearly had died and she felt as if something had just died inside her.

Colette heard Mrs Dell's voice faintly. Another

question had been asked but she could not grasp what it was. Although she tried to ask for the question to be repeated, no sound came from her lips. A crushing mixture of grief and guilt penetrated her and she could not speak. Colette slumped forward and for a moment thought she was going to black out. Instead she just sat paralysed on the hard wooden seat inside the witness box and cried. Once again she heard the sound of voices.

"Perhaps we should adjourn for a few minutes, Mrs Dell," Judge Flannery said. It was a statement rather than a question.

"That might be appropriate, judge," Mrs Dell dutifully responded as Mr Justice Flannery stood and walked quickly from the courtroom into the privacy of the judges' chambers at the back of the court, escaping the spectacle of the grief-torn witness.

Apart from the noise of Colette crying, there was no other sound. She took up in her hand the glass of water offered by Mrs Dell as Paul Galloway shuffled uncomfortably out of court to grant her some measure of privacy.

"I'll . . . I'll be alright in a minute. I'm sorry . . ." Colette said, mechanically drinking the water from the glass and trying to get a grip on herself.

"It's alright – just take a few minutes to recover and then we'll start again. Would you like to get some fresh air?" enquired Mrs Dell, genuine concern on her face.

"No, thank you. I'm okay now. I'm sorry. I didn't mean to break down like that. I'm not much help to you, am I?"

"Don't worry, you've done yourself no harm," Mrs Dell replied soothingly.

Ten minutes later the court resumed and Colette continued her evidence in reply to Mrs Dell's questions. Her decision to get Laura back, the visit to her parents, the phone call to St Mark's and the meeting with Mrs Comerford were all recounted.

"What attitude did Mrs Comerford take to you at that time?"

"Sympathetic – in fact she gave me more sympathy than I expected. She was also very questioning. She questioned everything I said. I suspected she disapproved of the idea of my taking Laura back."

"How did you feel after the meeting with her?"

"Confused initially, uncertain I think, but very soon after the meeting I was again sure that I wanted Laura back."

In response to further probing by Mrs Dell, Colette described her relationship with Michael O'Brien, the decision to start legal proceedings, her appendicitis and reconciliation with her parents.

As she came to the end of her evidence, Mrs Dell asked, "And what is your attitude to Laura now?"

"I want her back. I want my daughter back," Colette replied quickly.

"Why?"

"Because I love her and she is my daughter. If she was allowed time with me, she would quickly love me too."

Mrs Dell sat down and as she did so the judge looked at his watch.

"It's five minutes to one. Perhaps we should adjourn for lunch before Mr Galloway starts his cross-examination."

"Certainly, judge," Paul Galloway replied, half-rising from his seat.

As they all filed out of court Colette realised that she had been in the witness box for almost two hours. Galloway had sat silently in court during Colette's evidence, carefully noting down her every word. He knew that she had been a good witness and had made a favourable impression. It would be his turn to question her after lunch.

* * *

Galloway's cross-examination started at two o'clock and lasted for three quarters of an hour. His questioning was at all times quiet, occasionally sympathetic, but most of the time unsettling. It seemed to Colette that she was merely repeating much of what she had already said, yet somehow the emphasis was different.

"You decided on adoption for your baby before her birth, I think?"

"Yes, that's right."

"Immediately after her birth you again stated that you wanted her adopted?"

"Yes."

"And it was at your request that Mrs Comerford visited you in hospital?"

"Yes."

"And at all stages you understood what was meant by adoption – that you would be giving up your baby to another couple and that, upon an adoption order being made, you would legally cease to be your daughter's mother?"

"Yes, I suppose – I understood all of those things," Colette admitted.

"And you permitted the adoption process to continue for over eight months without interruption?"

"Yes, but I had no other choice. There was nothing else I could do."

"Could you not have taken your baby home with you or back to your flat?"

"At the time I thought that would be impossible. I was terrified my parents would find out about Laura if I did so."

"Was any alternative to adoption ever suggested to you?" Judge Flannery asked, interrupting the cross-examination.

"Well, Mrs Comerford suggested that Laura go from the hospital to a temporary foster home to give me more time to think things over, but I didn't want my baby to have to spend time temporarily in fosterage and then be passed on like a parcel to adopters. I believed that if I couldn't have her she should be with a family who really wanted her and would permanently care for her."

"I see," responded the judge. "I'm sorry for interrupting you, Mr Galloway. Please continue."

The cross-examination took Colette through her relationship with her parents and with Brannigan.

"You said you would not marry Laura's father and that you no longer had a relationship with him. At the time when you became pregnant, was Laura's father married or unmarried?"

"Married," she replied, shifting uncomfortably in her chair.

"And did his wife ever learn of your relationship with her husband?"

"No, I don't think so. He told me they didn't get on . . ." Her voice trailed off.

"Have you had a relationship with any other married men since then?"

"Objection," cried Mrs Dell, leaping to her feet. "Judge, any subsequent relationship the witness may or may not have had can be of no relevance to the issue before the court."

"Objection sustained. Now I really don't think that type of question is very relevant at this stage, Mr Galloway," Judge Flannery said disapprovingly.

"Very well, judge," Galloway said. Taking the reprimand in his stride and changing direction, he continued. "Yesterday, in their evidence, the adopters referred to the meeting that took place in St Mark's. Would you agree that Laura spent most of the time with the adopters and that after sitting on your lap for a brief period she became distressed?"

"She hardly knew me. The only other time I saw my daughter was the day she was born." Colette's voice rose. She was becoming irritated by Galloway's questioning.

"How do you think she would react if she was returned to you tomorrow or next week?"

"Well, I suppose she would be upset in the beginning but she would get over it. She is my daughter."

"You said that Laura's father offered you no help when you told him you were pregnant other than to suggest you should have an abortion."

"Yes, that's right – other than some help with medical expenses relating to Laura's birth, which I refused."

"Did he subsequently offer you any help?" Galloway asked.

"I wouldn't describe it as an offer," Colette answered.

"What did he do?" asked Galloway, a lawyer's cunning telling him that he might have hit on something important.

"Well, he eventually gave me money to help me bring this court case to get Laura back." Colette spoke uncertainly.

"How much did he give you, Miss James?" Galloway probed.

"Thirty-five thousand euro."

"And you did not bring court proceedings until you got this money from the father?"

Colette could feel the anger burning inside her.

"That's not true! My solicitor had already sent a

letter to St Mark's saying that I wanted Laura back. I had already decided to bring this court case. It was only at Michael O'Brien's suggestion that I sought financial help from the father."

"And do you expect any more . . . er . . . financial help from him?" Galloway asked.

"No, of course not!" Colette was shouting now. "What do you think I'm doing – blackmailing him?"

Galloway thanked the witness and sat down.

Judge Flannery glanced towards Mrs Dell. She got to her feet and looked straight at Colette.

"Would you have sought to regain custody of your daughter through the courts if you had received no money from Laura's father?" she asked, speaking with deliberation.

"Yes, of course I would have!" Colette sounded exasperated.

Mrs Dell sat down and Judge Flannery turned to Colette.

"Thank you, Miss James, there appear to be no further questions."

Colette stood up and returned slowly to her seat. Any optimism she had felt at the conclusion of Mrs Dell's questions in the morning was now totally extinguished. The rest of the hearing, she knew now, was merely a sham. She told herself that she would remain in the courtroom for the rest of that day and watch the proceedings march relentlessly towards what she knew was the inevitable result: the judge would refuse to return Laura to her. But she no longer cared what the court would decide. She comforted herself with the knowledge that neither her own nor Laura's future would ultimately depend on the judgement that would be delivered by Mr Justice Flannery.

twenty

Mrs Comerford followed Colette into the witness box. In reply to Mrs Dell's questions, she gave a sympathetic description of her dealings with Colette.

"I was satisfied that when she agreed to the placement of Laura with adopters, Colette fully understood the implications of what she was doing."

"Is five days after a child's birth not very soon for a mother to sign a form agreeing to an adoption placement?" Mrs Dell asked.

"It's fairly early, but not all that unusual. Many young mothers whose families are unaware of a pregnancy insist on an early agreement to place. In some instances, if the parents are aware of a pregnancy, they try to force an unmarried daughter into agreeing quickly to adoption, but that didn't arise in this case."

"And did you do anything to suggest that matters might be delayed?"

"I did suggest the baby might be placed in a foster home, but Colette was totally against that. It wasn't a question of forcing Colette to have Laura adopted – she was forcing the pace herself."

"How would you describe her mood at that time?"

"I think she was distressed but fairly certain of what she wanted to do."

"Did you suggest any other options to her, such as Laura being placed temporarily in a children's home?"

"No. She kept on pushing for adoption."

"Is it possible she might have agreed to a children's home?"

"I suppose it's *possible* but I do not believe it likely. Her main anxiety seemed to be to conceal her pregnancy from her parents. I tried to talk her into telling them about it before making any final decisions but she refused to do so."

"You visited Colette twice in hospital?"

"Yes. The hospital registrar telephoned me after the baby was born and I visited her a couple of days later and again the day she was to leave hospital."

"And what happened during those visits?"

"She insisted that she wanted the baby adopted," replied Mrs Comerford. "I suggested that she should give herself a bit more time but she was insistent."

"How was she during those visits?"

"Well, she seemed very tense. On one occasion she got very upset when a nurse came in and suggested that she see her baby."

"Why do you think she reacted that way?"

"I'm not sure. I thought at the time that she was afraid to see the baby."

"What do you mean by that?"

"I felt that she was frightened that if she saw the baby again she might not agree to its going to adopters. I think she was trying to close her mind to what had happened. I tried to persuade her to see the baby again before she signed the adoption papers, but she refused."

Mrs Dell's questioning continued.

Mrs Comerford denied that she had been in any way obstructive when Colette had told her of her desire to have Laura returned to her.

"I just wanted to be sure that Colette understood what she would be taking on if her request was complied with. I was also anxious to ensure that she really knew what she wanted to do before the adopters were told, as I realised how much distress they would be caused if they learned of Colette's change of mind. I knew they would be heartbroken."

Mrs Dell sat down and it was Paul Galloway's turn to cross-examine Mrs Comerford.

"How long have you worked for St Mark's, Mrs Comerford?"

"For almost fifteen years."

"During that time you would have been involved as a social worker with many mothers who have arranged to have their babies adopted."

"Yes, Mr Galloway, a great many."

"When signing adoption papers and agreeing to

their babies being adopted, have most of these mothers done so happily, or would you say that most of them have been distressed on such occasions?"

"I suppose most of them have been distressed . . . some of them have been very distressed."

"Would you agree that, at the time Colette James agreed to the adoption of her child, she was no more distressed than most mothers are in such circumstances?"

"I suppose so. I couldn't say her reaction was very different to that of a number of other mothers I have been involved with."

"You would agree it was not exceptional?"

"It was not all that unusual."

"And when she signed the adoption papers, did she know and understand what she was doing?"

"I was very careful to explain the implications of it all to her. I had in fact done so already when she came to St Mark's before the baby was born, but I always go over things again prior to the mother signing the placement form. In the hospital she became somewhat irritated at my repeating it all."

Galloway sat down. Judge Flannery looked towards Mrs Dell, his glance enquiring whether there were any further questions she wished to ask arising from Galloway's cross-examination. Mrs Dell remained seated, realising that there was really nothing more she could ask that would be certain to elicit replies that would be helpful to her client.

Sally Thomas then came to the witness stand and

vividly described Colette's behaviour and state of mind during the time they lived together.

"For some months after the birth she was fine and nothing seemed to bother her. Then suddenly she became weepy and refused to talk to anybody. She kept me up all hours of the night, crying in her sleep, talking about her baby. I really didn't know what to do about her. It was only after she decided to go to court that she seemed to settle down again."

Bill and Margaret James, Colette's parents, were also called to give evidence. They both expressed their love for their daughter.

"If only she had told us earlier," Colette's mother said, but then agreed that if she had done so, her reaction and that of her husband would not necessarily have been any different to the reaction Sally Thomas had witnessed when she had told them about Colette's baby.

After Colette's parents had given evidence, Michael O'Brien was called to the witness stand. Although he had been a TD for over a year, he still felt uneasy when standing up in the Dáil to deliver a speech. The same feeling of unease affected him as he sat down in the witness box after taking the oath. In response to Mrs Dell's questions he gave an account of what he knew of Colette since she had started working for him. Much of his evidence confirmed the account that she herself had already given. He described his meeting with her when she finally told him about the existence of Laura and how Robert Barnes, at his request, had agreed to see her that day. Michael O'Brien then related his encounter with Laura's father without revealing his identity and concluded his initial evidence: "I believe that Colette was confused when she agreed to place her child for adoption. I believe she was scared of her parents' reaction and did not fully understand what she was doing. I think the fact that the father of her child and her father were friends added to her difficulties."

"Please reply to Mr Galloway's questions," said Mrs Dell as she sat down.

Galloway stood up, one foot resting on his chair, the other firmly on the ground. He looked straight at Michael O'Brien.

"Deputy O'Brien, you did not know Colette James at the time of her pregnancy – is that correct?"

"It is."

"You did not meet her until some weeks after she had given birth, isn't that also correct?"

"Yes, it is."

"In fact you knew nothing of her baby until many months after Colette James became your secretary and you started socialising. Is that so?"

"Yes, I suppose so," Michael O'Brien replied, understanding where the questions were leading.

"So you are not in a position to give evidence to this court as to Colette's state of mind when she agreed to place her child for adoption. Would that be a fair assumption?"

"To some extent you are right, but from what I have since learned about what happened I believe that

Colette did not at that time really understand or think through what she was doing."

Galloway pounced. "Is this not what could be described as a retrospective rationalisation of what occurred?"

"I beg your pardon, could you repeat that?" asked Michael O'Brien, floundering.

"There is no need for you to do so," interrupted Judge Flannery. "I think this is one of the central issues upon which I must give judgement, Mr Galloway. There is no need to pursue this issue any further with this witness. It is clear that he did not know Miss James at the time the baby was placed for adoption."

"Very well, judge," replied Galloway, knowing that the point he was making had been understood.

The cross-examination continued.

"If you had not taken Miss James to a solicitor, do you think she would have pursued matters this far?"

"I believe she would have done so. She was distraught, she wanted her daughter back and she was looking for help. If I had not arranged the appointment with Robert Barnes for her, I'm sure she would have turned to someone else for help and found another lawyer."

Galloway explored Michael O'Brien's role in the raising of the thirty-five thousand euro and for the second time Michael had to describe his meeting with Brannigan. He referred to him as a "member of the Dáil" but avoided revealing his identity. To satisfy his own curiosity, Galloway would have liked to discover the identity of the anonymous Dáil Deputy who had fathered Laura and who had obviously abandoned her mother, but he knew that pressing this issue was not going to help the Mastersons and might antagonise the judge, who had already decided that the father's identity was irrelevant. Galloway, however, felt that there might be more behind the payment of thirty-five thousand euro than had yet emerged.

"Whose idea was it to get money from this anonymous TD?"

"It was mine."

"You're quite sure Miss James did not suggest to you that this man could be blackmailed out of this money?"

"This is outrageous," O'Brien retorted, restraining his anger with difficulty.

"If Colette James succeeded in having this court return her daughter to her, would this TD not become a permanent mark for her financial demands?"

"He has my word and that of Colette James that this will not happen."

"I'm sorry, Deputy O'Brien, but I must suggest to you that despite your word and that of Miss James, it could happen. If Miss James wins this case, this TD could become the victim of Miss James' blackmail and I must suggest to you that her desire to recover her child is not solely motivated by feelings of love for her daughter but partly by a desire to exact revenge on her daughter's father. Is that not so?"

Judge Flannery intervened.

"I don't think this line of questioning is of any help to your clients, Mr Galloway," he snapped. "I am quite satisfied that Miss James is not motivated by any desire to blackmail the father."

"Very well. I'm sorry, judge. I have no further questions." Galloway slowly sat down, realising that he might have gone too far. Unlike some of his judicial colleagues Judge Flannery was a courteous and kindly man and was not normally so abrupt. Galloway hoped that the last line of questioning he had pursued would not reflect badly on the Mastersons.

Michael O'Brien left the witness box and rejoined the other witnesses sitting in the waiting room.

"My final witness, judge, is Dr Lloyd," announced Mrs Dell as Robert Barnes showed the doctor into the courtroom and directed him towards the witness box.

Dr Lloyd recited his qualifications to the court and identified his assessment report, a copy of which was handed to the judge. Like Dr O'Connell's report, it confirmed that Laura had bonded with the Mastersons.

"Until relatively recently it was believed that there was an instinctual relationship between a biological mother and her child, is that not so, doctor?" asked Mrs Dell.

"Yes, that is true, but studies over the past thirty-five years have emphasised the importance of the psychological as opposed to the biological parents."

"A lot of this is still theory, is it not?"

"It is based on an analysis of the effect on children of the breaking of bonds or attachments."

"Is there a magical moment in a child's life when one can say that bonds or attachments have been fully formed? Is it after three months, six months, one year, two years?"

"It all depends on the parenting of the child. If a baby has experienced continuous parenting with one couple for over a year, it can be predicted that bonds have been formed. If these bonds are broken, in the short term a child's development may be retarded."

"So the evidence you give is predictive, not certain?"

"Well, one cannot be definite about every child. I can only give evidence as to the general effect on a child's development of the breaking of bonds. Some children may be affected more than others."

"You are in fact looking into a psychological crystal ball and trying to predict the future?" Mrs Dell probed just as she had done with Dr O'Connell.

"To some extent that is true."

"There are children who at a very young age become orphans, are brought up by people other than their biological parents and develop normally. Is that not so?"

"That is so."

"If this particular child were transferred from the adopters to the biological mother, what short-term impact do you believe it would have on her, doctor?"

"The child would, I believe, suffer some initial stress and her development would be retarded in the short term. If, however, she were provided with the loving and caring environment that every child needs for its proper development by her mother and her grandparents, there is no reason to suppose that the child would not then form new bonds or attachments and develop normally."

"What about the long-term consequences of this for the child?"

"That is more difficult to predict. She might be at risk of some long-term damage but not necessarily so."

"Dr O'Connell was certain that long-term damage would result. Can you also be so certain?"

"No, I cannot."

"Finally, doctor, from the assessment you have carried out, is Colette James an unfit or unsuitable person to mother and care for her own child?"

"No, of course she isn't."

"Thank you, Dr Lloyd."

Mrs Dell sat down and Galloway stood up for his final cross-examination. He decided to be brief.

"Do you believe, doctor, that it is in the best interests of Laura that she remain with the adopters or do you believe she should be given back to her mother?"

"That is very difficult to say."

"Why?"

"Well, I have no doubt that if she is removed from the adopters, she will suffer immediate feelings of loss which, as I have already said, will retard her short-term development. I cannot, however, be definite about the long-term consequences. It is very difficult to predict whether this particular child might be better off in the long term with her biological mother or with the adopters. I simply do not know."

"If the child, Laura, is allowed to remain with the adopters, the short-term consequences that will result from her being removed from the woman she now regards as her mother will not arise. Is that not so, doctor?" asked Galloway.

"That is correct."

"Therefore, doctor, is it not in the child's short-term interests that she remain with the adopters?"

"What you say is correct but what it all means for the child's long-term welfare I cannot say."

"Finally, could I ask you again about the orphan analogy mentioned by Mrs Dell. I suggest to you that this analogy is not relevant to this case because a child rendered an orphan may lose its parents but will in most cases retain and build on relationships with the extended family, such as aunts and uncles, and with various family friends. However, if the child in question here is transferred to the biological mother, she will not only lose her psychological parents but her relationship with the entire extended family will also end abruptly. Does that not place her in a different position from an orphan such as Mrs Dell referred to?"

"That is so." Dr Lloyd's response was noticeably brief.

Galloway sat down, satisfied that he had scored some points that would help the Mastersons. Though Dr Lloyd, as the mother's witness, was doing everything he could to be of help to the mother, Galloway nevertheless believed that his evidence had not greatly advanced the mother's case.

As Dr Lloyd stood up to leave the witness box, Judge Flannery spoke to him.

"Just one more question, doctor, with reference to the possible long-term damage that could result if the child were to be returned to her biological mother. We regularly hear nowadays of adopted children trying to trace their origin or roots and suffering crises of identity. If this child remained with the adopters and at a later stage in her life learned that her mother had sought to prevent her adoption and had been opposed by the adopters, could this not create a serious crisis in her life with resultant psychological damage?"

"That is possible. The effect of such a revelation would very much depend on the age of the child and the circumstances of her being told. I'm not familiar with any studies into this issue. I cannot rule out harmful consequences."

"So would I be right in saying, doctor, that there is no ideal prescription for the future care of this child?"

"That is one way of putting it."

"Thank you, doctor. You have been most helpful."

The judge gestured to Dr Lloyd to leave the witness box.

As he stepped down, Colette stood up and shouted, "Laura is my daughter! You're supposed to be on my side. You are supposed to get her back for me. Tell the judge she should be returned to me!"

Robert Barnes quickly rose and went over to Colette, who was now crying. She lashed out at him with her hands as he attempted to calm her. Then she collapsed onto the floor. Barnes helped her up and back onto her seat.

Mrs Dell stood up.

"I'm sorry, judge," she muttered.

"It's alright, Mrs Dell, I understand. These cases are distressing for everyone."

"That completes my evidence, judge," Mrs Dell said.

The judge looked up at the clock, which showed four thirty-five.

"I think we shall postpone legal submissions and arguments until tomorrow. Say ten in the morning to ensure we get finished in one day."

"If you please," chorused Galloway and Dell.

"There will be no submissions on behalf of the Adoption Authority," announced the Authority's counsel, who had sat silently throughout the day's proceedings.

Judge Flannery rose to leave the room and all the lawyers stood up and bowed. Robert Barnes helped Colette James into the consultation room adjacent to the court and recounted the day's events to her parents, Sally Thomas and Michael O'Brien, who were all waiting there.

Paul Galloway rushed back to his office to contact the Mastersons who, he knew, would be waiting anxiously beside their phone to hear how the case was progressing. The last series of questions put by the judge to Dr Lloyd had made him feel uneasy but he decided not to communicate his disquiet to the Mastersons. He would merely tell them that the day had gone as well as could be expected but that he still could not predict the result with certainty.

As Galloway drove over O'Connell Bridge towards his office, he absentmindedly read a billboard advertisement that was leaning against a lamp-post. It was for the latest edition of the *Evening Herald*: 5,000 IRISH UK ABORTIONS – BRANNIGAN CALLS FOR GOVERNMENT ACTION, the placard bellowed, reproducing that evening's main headline.

Fifteen minutes earlier Colette James had shuddered as she, too, read the billboard from the front seat of Michael O'Brien's car. He was driving Colette and her parents home from the courtroom in Ó'Dálaigh House.

twenty-one

Seán Brannigan was dumbfounded when he read the front-page headline of the *Evening Herald*. Ever since his confrontation with Michael O'Brien he had steered clear of involving himself in any public controversy. He had turned down numerous invitations to speak at public meetings and to participate in university debates, including even an invitation from the Historical Society of Trinity College Dublin to propose a motion "That this House would uphold Irish moral values". The students had hoped he would be their star turn.

Although he had not talked to Colette James since the birth of their child, he had kept in touch with what was happening through Bill James, Colette's father, who still did not know that Brannigan was the father of his only grandchild. When Bill James learned of the birth of his daughter's baby, his local TD was the first person to whom he turned for advice and help.

"Surely you must have known she was pregnant, Seán? She was your secretary at the time?" asked Bill James one day after Sally and Colette's traumatic visits to his home.

"I really didn't know, Bill," the TD responded without any hesitation. "I just thought she was putting on a little weight. This is as big a shock to me as it is to you."

In response to further questions from Bill James, Brannigan persistently maintained that he could shed no light on the identity of the child's father. In the weeks that followed, Bill James visited Brannigan on a weekly basis to unburden himself. Brannigan's great fear was that Colette might reveal his part in the family drama to her parents. Although this fear proved groundless, he found the discussions with her father a nerve-racking ordeal. It suited him that father and daughter were no longer on speaking terms, yet when pressed for advice by his troubled friend about what he should do, Brannigan felt that he had no choice but to encourage him to make contact with Colette.

"You can't just cut her out of your lives permanently, Bill. She's your only child. Perhaps you should give yourself and Margaret a little time to come to terms with the situation and then go to visit her or phone her and ask her to come home to discuss things."

After a time the anxiety Brannigan felt before each meeting with Bill James intensified into a feeling

186

of dread as he found himself being further trapped in a web of deceit from which he could not disentangle himself. He cut down on the number of local political party meetings that he attended. He wanted to avoid the inevitable whispered conversation with Bill James over a beer in the bar at the end of the meeting. His regular phone calls to Brannigan's home terrified him in case his wife started to grow suspicious, although he knew that, rationally speaking, there was no reason why she should. He and James had phoned each other regularly for years to talk local politics. Yet somehow the frequent messages asking that he phone Colette's father never ceased to trouble him. Each time he dialled the James' home, he was apprehensive that Colette might have revealed the identity of the father of her child to her distraught parents.

To avoid arousing suspicion, in the months following the birth of Laura, Brannigan continued with what he politically described as his moral crusade, although he spent far more time than had been his habit on local constituency work and a good deal less time on the preparation and delivery of controversial political speeches. He avoided the issues of abortion and divorce and instead took a public stance against homosexuality. There was talk of a constitutional amendment to allow same-sex couples to marry and Brannigan alleged that this could be forced on the Irish people by the European Court. Years earlier that court had declared that Irish laws which criminalised homosexual intimacy were in violation of the European Convention on Human Rights and such laws had been repealed. Denouncing homosexuality and those campaigning for gay marriage, Brannigan declared that God himself had given an unmistakable sign to the Irish people and to the European Court that traditional moral values should be upheld. "God's wrath at the European Court's stance and his detestation of unnatural sexual acts have been made clear by the plague of AIDS that is sweeping America and Europe. AIDS is God's signal that gay marriage must not be accepted or tolerated in Ireland!" Brannigan thundered. He conveniently chose to ignore that his political colleagues on all sides in the Dáil had largely ignored his views three years earlier, enacting legislation to facilitate gay partners enter into civil partnerships which could be regarded as marriages in everything but name.

The public controversy generated by Brannigan's "Wrath of God speech" was greeted with wry amusement by two members of the Leinster House secretariat between whom the birth of Brannigan's fourth child, and Colette's first, was still a major talking point.

"It is good to note that our TD from Dublin West-Central will never suffer the Wrath of God," remarked Maeve O'Doherty to Sally Thomas over coffee the morning after the speech had been delivered. Maeve O'Doherty was Michael O'Brien's temporary secretary.

On that same day Michael O'Brien had visited

Brannigan to tell him of Colette's decision to fight for the custody of their daughter in the courts. As O'Brien walked out of the room and closed the door behind him, their confrontation ended and the deal agreed, Brannigan was sitting limply at his desk. In a state of shock he reached forward to answer the ringing phone.

"Is that you, Seán?" Bill James asked before the phone line went dead.

Unknown to Colette's father, Brannigan, by now totally unnerved, had at that moment disconnected the telephone wire. With the words "Wrath of God" echoing in his ears, he remained sitting inertly at his desk, gazing blindly out of the window of his office at the two ducks swimming peacefully in the small pond in the garden at the back of Leinster House.

* * *

An early morning phone call to Seán Brannigan's home by a reporter manning the *Evening Herald* newsdesk was the cause of the headline that Colette and the others saw as they were driving from court. There was little happening that morning and the print run for the early edition of the paper needed a good headline. Just after eight o'clock the latest statistics on the number of Irish women who had undergone abortions in England became available. A comment from Brannigan on the statistics and the *Herald* would have its lead story.

* * *

Seán Brannigan had been up for almost two hours when the phone rang. He knew it was the start of the second day of the court case. Colette and her parents were fully reconciled and Bill James had been on the phone to him the previous evening, passing on to him the lawyer's account of the first day in court.

"I just do not understand why Colette won't tell us who the father is," Bill James said. "He might be willing to give evidence that would be helpful to Colette. She just says their relationship is over, that he is already married and that he has no interest in her or the baby."

"She must have good reasons for approaching matters this way, Bill," Brannigan responded. "She is under enough pressure as it is. I don't think you should put her under any more. I'm sure she's discussed all this with her lawyers."

"I suppose you're right," Bill James had answered uncertainly.

His telephone conversation with Colette's father had haunted Brannigan throughout the night. As his wife lay sound asleep beside him, he dozed fretfully, Bill James' words echoing and re-echoing in his head. Was there something he could do to help Colette? Could his own cowardice result not only in her losing her child but would it also destroy her life? She was not the first girl with whom he'd had a sexual fling, but he had not been so close to the others. He had not watched them growing up as he had done Colette. Nor had he been close to their parents. He must have been mad to have let things go so far. Now he knew he had to protect himself, but was he destroying them both by abandoning her?

When the newspapers were delivered through his letterbox just after six o'clock that morning Seán Brannigan had an excuse for getting out of bed. When the reporter's call came shortly after eight he had not only read his three morning papers from cover to cover but had also opened and read all the early morning emails and had already dealt with phone calls from three constituents.

"Have you heard the latest abortion statistics?" enquired the reporter, whose name Brannigan failed to catch.

"No, I haven't," he replied, immediately regretting having answered the phone.

"According to figures just published, over five thousand Irish women obtained abortions in the UK over the last twelve months. Have you any comment?" The reporter was eager to get some answer from Brannigan.

"Well, er . . . these are new figures, are they?" asked Brannigan, playing for time.

"Just published, too late for the morning papers," came the swift response.

Brannigan realised that he was caught and had to say something. If only he hadn't answered the phone.

"Have you any comment?" repeated the persistent reporter.

"The figures are shocking," Brannigan curtly answered.

"Would you like the Government to take any action?"

"I have already said that they should act," Brannigan replied with a note of irritation in his voice.

"Is there anything else you wish to add?"

Brannigan hastily invented a reason to escape his questioner. "I don't think so. I'm sorry for cutting you off, but there is a family matter I must deal with."

"Oh, that's okay," replied the reporter, satisfied now he had his headline. "I'm sorry for ringing you so early, Deputy. Thanks very much for your comments."

The phone went dead and Brannigan, feeling weak, hand shaking, put down the receiver. Today of all days he had no wish to be reported on the issue of abortion. What effect would a newspaper report carrying his ritual condemnation of the Government's failure to prevent Irish girls having abortions in the UK have on Colette, he wondered. Thankfully the conversation with the reporter had been brief.

There's not much they can quote in that, Brannigan consoled himself. He was wrong.

* * *

Seán Brannigan's brief encounter with the reporter from the *Herald* caught up with him later in the day. That evening, as he drove to a political meeting, the headline, reproduced on countless newspaper billboards all over Dublin, followed him along his route through the city. When he arrived at the public house where the meeting was to take place, it had already started. A copy of the evening paper, splashed with Guinness, was already spread out on the table at which he had to sit with the members of his local political organisation. His own supporters were accustomed to reading about his attacks on the Government over the issue of abortion and thankfully had other things on their minds.

As he sat there, Brannigan was oblivious of the criticisms his supporters were voicing about the numbers unemployed and forced to emigrate and the Government's failure to tackle the problem. He was miles away. He had not talked to Bill James on the phone that evening and did not know how the court case had gone during the day. Relief at avoiding the ordeal of another difficult phone discussion was counterbalanced by a desire to know what had happened in court. Brannigan was terrified that Colette might have revealed his role in fathering Laura while giving evidence, but he also realised that even if she had not done so, he could not live in fear for the rest of his life that one day she might give him away, either deliberately or by accident. Brannigan's thoughts were in turmoil. Deaf to the heated political debate going on around him, he sank deeper and deeper into a morass of guilt. It was his fault that Colette had become pregnant. He should have taken proper precautions or encouraged her to do so. If only he had been more considerate when he had learned of her pregnancy she might have decided to keep her baby – their baby – right from the start and not placed it for adoption.

Seán Brannigan now realised that he could no longer pretend that he was not involved in the courtroom battle that was being fought over Laura's future at Ó'Dálaigh House.

twenty-two

Paul Galloway lay in bed, unable to sleep. It was three o'clock in the morning. He had spent two hours that night revising the legal submissions he had originally prepared to make to the court as soon as the witnesses had completed their oral evidence. Now he tried unsuccessfully to shut the day's events out of his mind.

Galloway had been specialising in family law for over ten years and rarely brought his clients' problems home with him. Adoption disputes were always the exception. There was a devastating finality about the decision made by a court when determining such disputes. They were very different to the custody cases that took place between estranged parents after a failed marriage. A parent deprived of custody was almost always granted visitation rights and could maintain a relationship and spend time with his or her child. In most cases the child could still have a relationship with

195

both parents, although on occasion animosity between the parents made this difficult.

Adoption disputes were different. A decision either to allow or to refuse to permit the making of an adoption order usually cut off the child entirely from either its biological mother or prospective adopters to whom it was attached. One side not alone lost a legal battle but had the child whom they loved removed completely from their lives. Galloway had no doubt that Laura should be allowed to remain with the Mastersons. Nevertheless, having seen and cross-examined Colette James in the witness box, he had felt the pain in her voice and had been touched by her anguish. Privately he acknowledged that her love for Laura was no less real than that of the Mastersons. It was clear to Galloway that Judge Flannery's assessment of Colette James did not differ greatly from his own. No one could doubt that she now deeply regretted handing Laura over to adopters and that if she lost the case she would probably never forgive herself for giving up her baby.

Galloway found it impossible to predict whether the judge would regard Colette's decision to place Laura up for adoption as valid or invalid. It all depended on whether he believed that she had freely decided on adoption, fully understanding the consequences of her actions, or whether he thought that she was too distressed to make such a decision voluntarily or to understand what she was doing. If her decision to have Laura adopted was held to be invalid, no adoption order could be made. If it was held to be valid, the judge had to be satisfied it was in Laura's best interests that she remain with the adopters before the court could permit her adoption.

On the basis of the welfare reports and much of the psychiatric evidence, Galloway believed that if the first hurdle – getting Colette's original decision recognised as valid – was cleared, the Mastersons would ultimately be successful in having an adoption order made in their favour. The judge's final questions to Dr Lloyd, however, had left Galloway with a nagging doubt.

He lay in bed as quietly as possible and tried to sleep, telling himself that he would be of no use in court later that morning without some rest. He heard crying and jumped out of bed before his wife awoke. Lifting Daniel, his fourteen-month-old son, out of his cot he cradled him in his arms.

"Shush, it's Daddy, you're having a dream, shush," he said, gently rocking the small child from side to side and then carefully lowering him back into his cot.

Daniel lay on his side and fell back into an untroubled sleep. For a few minutes Galloway stood beside the cot watching him.

"I love you, little boy," he muttered to himself and then silently walked out of the child's room and back into his own bedroom. He climbed back into his bed and fell into a restless sleep.

At six in the morning he awoke with a start, his back wet with perspiration. He sat up, slowly recognising the familiar pattern of the bedroom curtain. Heaving a sigh of relief, he lay back down, putting his arms around his sleeping wife and kissing her gently on the back of her neck. Paul Galloway had had a nightmare in which an elderly woman resembling Imelda Hennessy, accompanied by a man in uniform, had arrived at his house and had forcibly removed Daniel. Imelda Hennessy mockingly told him that he would never see his son again. Each time he tried to stand up in a courtroom before Judge Flannery to ask him to order Daniel's return, he spoke in a legal gibberish that only he understood. The judge, believing him to be drunk, ordered his removal from the court. Galloway woke up as two burly guards were carrying him screaming from the courtroom.

As he lay awake in bed, staring at the familiar patterned curtains, Paul Galloway wondered how Jenny or John Masterson or Colette James had been able to retain their sanity. He doubted if he would do so if forced to live through their ordeal.

* * *

John and Jenny Masterson were drinking a third cup of coffee. It was five thirty in the morning and they had been awake for most of the night. Something in Galloway's account of the day's events in court had increased their feelings of anxiety. Neither of them could pinpoint what it was. Both of them had talked to him on the phone and he had given each of them practically identical accounts of what had happened in court.

"It was something in his voice," Jenny explained. "He seemed less sure of himself. Less confident."

"Maybe it's us," John replied. "Maybe we're getting a little paranoid."

"I don't know. I wish we could have been in court. And it's going to last another day. I'd feel better if I could just see and hear everything for myself."

"I suppose the mother feels the same way."

"To hell with the mother!" Jenny became angry. "If it weren't for her, none of this would be happening."

"If it wasn't for her, we wouldn't have had Laura in the first place," John replied calmly. "There's no point in going over it all again. We'll soon know the outcome. There's nothing more we can do now, Jenny. It all depends on the lawyers and the judge."

They both fell silent. Upstairs, her bedroom door closed, Laura slept soundly, watched over by the hundreds of brown teddy-bears that looked down at her from the papered walls. Outside her door, curled in a foetal ball, Rebel lay softly snoring, lost in night-time canine fantasies. In the dark garden a cat wailed a promiscuous night song. It was in heat and looking for a mate. Neither John nor Jenny heard it; both were deaf to the outside world, their inner world and thoughts concentrated on Laura, both silently praying that she would be allowed to remain with them.

* * *

Colette James, exhausted by the day's events, fell into a deep sleep. For her the next day's court hearing and the judge's decision were no longer relevant. She knew that she could no longer rely on others. Laura's future was going to be determined by her and by no one else.

twenty-three

Robert Barnes was finishing his breakfast-time cup of coffee and glancing at the headlines in the morning paper when the phone rang.

"Hello, is Robert Barnes there?"

There was something familiar about the voice, but Barnes could not identify the speaker.

"Robert Barnes speaking."

"Seán Brannigan, Deputy Seán Brannigan here. I'm sorry for disturbing you. I'm ringing about Colette James. Would it be possible for me to see you this morning before you go to court?"

Barnes now knew why he recognised the voice. It was because he had heard it on so many news and current affairs broadcasts. He had been surprised to learn the identity of Laura's father. The deal which had been done between Brannigan and Michael O'Brien had never required that Barnes meet with Brannigan directly or talk to him. It had all been arranged through an exchange of letters. He was puzzled that Brannigan was now in a hurry to see him and had no great desire to meet this man who, he thought, had treated Colette James so shabbily.

"Is it necessary that we meet today?" he asked cautiously, uncertain whether Brannigan knew that Colette's court case was continuing that day.

"I know that the Colette James' case is on again this morning. I'm phoning because I may be able to help her. I really feel that we should talk and it will be too late when the case is over."

Barnes was unsure how Brannigan could help but, anxious that every avenue be explored, he arranged to meet him at his office thirty minutes later. The court hearing was to resume at ten that morning.

When Barnes arrived at his office, Brannigan was already sitting in the reception area. Barnes greeted him and brought him up the stairs and into his room. They both sat down.

"Well, Deputy, what do you wish to discuss with me?" enquired Barnes, trying to disguise the disdain he felt towards Brannigan.

"How is Colette's case going so far?" enquired Brannigan.

"It's difficult to predict what will happen." Barnes was anxious not to reveal much.

"Is she going to get her child back?"

"I don't know," replied Barnes cautiously. "I'm not sure at this stage what the judge is thinking. The fact that the child has been with the adopters for over fourteen months creates a problem. If we can convince the judge that Colette was under so much stress when she agreed to place the baby with adopters that she was incapable of making a rational decision, we should succeed. But if the judge believes that Colette knew what she was doing, we will be in considerable difficulty."

"Am I correct in assuming that Colette has not told the court that I am the father of her child?"

"Colette has kept to the agreement she made with you," Barnes replied curtly, suspecting that Brannigan's anxiety about his own position was the reason for his pressing for this meeting.

"Would it help if I gave evidence on Colette's behalf?"

Robert Barnes was taken aback by this unexpected proposal. Up to that moment Brannigan's sole concern in the affair had apparently been to conceal his own involvement. Now he was offering to come to court and give evidence. Why was Brannigan coming forward in this way? Even if he did give evidence what value would it have?

Glancing at the clock, Barnes realised that he did not have time to explore Brannigan's motives. If he was to give evidence, Mrs Dell would be the first person to put questions to him in the witness box. Barnes phoned her and arranged that they would meet in a consultation room at Ó'Dálaigh House twenty minutes later. There Mrs Dell could consider what Brannigan had to say and the decision could be made whether or not he should be called as a witness. Although the judge had been told the previous day that no more witnesses were to be called on Colette James' behalf, fortunately legal submissions had not yet commenced. It was still possible for Judge Flannery to agree to an additional witness being called and a very rapid decision was going to have to be made whether Brannigan's unexpected offer should be accepted.

* * *

Paul Galloway was the first to arrive in the courtroom that morning. He spread out his legal volumes in front of him, careful to arrange them in the order in which he would make reference to their contents. The green-bound volumes of the *Irish Reports* and the loose volumes of the *Irish Law Reports Monthly* recorded the legal principles pronounced and relied upon by judges in many of the adoption and custody cases that had been previously determined. That morning they provided him with the legal meat upon which he would base the courtroom submissions which were designed to convince Judge Flannery to decide in favour of the Mastersons. In theory, he was making legal submissions "to assist" the judge in making his decision. In reality, he hoped to persuade the judge that a correct application of existing law could lead to only one conclusion – that Colette James had validly agreed to Laura's placement for adoption and that it was in

Laura's best interests that the Adoption Authority be permitted to make an adoption order.

Galloway knew that he had to apply a cold, clinical and objective legal analysis to the evidence heard by the judge. A mere emotional appeal to him to decide in favour of the Mastersons would be of no help. He also knew that it was possible that the judge might already have made his decision and that all of those who were to play a central part in that day's court proceedings might be simply role-playing, principal actors in a legal drama, who had to deliver their final lines before the judicial curtain came down.

The Adoption Authority's lawyers took their place at the table facing the judge's chair and just before ten o'clock Robert Barnes hurried into the courtroom, followed by Mrs Dell. Five minutes earlier, Colette James' junior barrister had arrived carrying the volumes of law reports Mrs Dell intended to use in legal argument. As Mrs Dell sat down, the judge entered. The lawyers stood and bowed.

"Good morning," said Judge Flannery, gesturing to them all to be seated as he took his place behind the registrar.

"James versus the Adoption Authority and Jennifer and John Masterson," called the registrar, announcing the business of the court for that day.

"I think we completed the oral evidence yesterday evening and we are now to start legal submissions. Is that correct?" asked the judge.

Mrs Dell stood up.

"Judge," she intoned, "there has been an unexpected development since the court adjourned. I stated yesterday that we had completed our evidence. This morning another witness came forward on behalf of Miss James and offered to give evidence. I have considered the evidence that this witness can give and, although I have not had time to consider it all in detail, I believe that the court should also be given the opportunity to hear this evidence and assess its relevance and importance. Unfortunately, I have not had time to warn my friend Mr Galloway, who is appearing for the Mastersons, of this development. I am, nevertheless, asking the court's permission to call a further witness before we embark on legal argument."

"What have you got to say, Mr Galloway?" asked the judge.

Mrs Dell had been careful not to reveal the identity of the witness or the exact nature of the evidence that this new witness could offer. Since legal argument had not yet commenced, Galloway thought it inevitable that the judge would grant Mrs Dell's application.

"I have no objection to Mrs Dell calling a further witness, judge. Since I do not know the nature of the evidence that is to be presented, it is possible that I may require time to consider its implications before the commencement of legal submissions, in particular if anything arises in relation to which I should obtain my clients' instructions."

"I think that's reasonable," said the judge. "The

Adoption Authority doesn't have any objections to this witness being called, does it, Mr Owen?"

"It does not," came the response from the Authority's senior counsel.

"Very well, Mrs Dell, call your witness," said Judge Flannery.

"I call Seán Brannigan TD," announced Mrs Dell as Robert Barnes hurried out to the adjacent consultation room where Brannigan was waiting.

As Brannigan stood in the witness box to take the oath, Barnes realised that he had not had time to phone Colette James to tell her of the morning's dramatic developments. He knew that he should have sought her instructions to ascertain whether she was agreeable to Brannigan being called as a witness, but he was not unduly concerned as he felt she would have relied on his advice and that of Mrs Dell in deciding what should be done. Both he and Mrs Dell, having heard in outline what Brannigan was going to say, had decided that his offer to give evidence should be accepted.

Brannigan took the oath and sat down. Mrs Dell stood up to question him and his evidence began.

"You were first elected as a TD for Dublin West-Central over sixteen years ago and you have been re-elected at successive general elections since then. Is that correct?"

"Yes."

"You are forty-seven years of age?"

"Yes."

"You are married and there are three children of your marriage?"

"Yes."

"I think you know Colette James?"

"I have known her since she was about six years old," he replied. "Her father, Bill James, has been a close friend for many years. He helped me to obtain my first nomination as a Dáil candidate for a general election. I have visited the James family's home regularly over the years and I watched Colette growing up. From an early age Colette helped out at election time. Well before she was a teenager, she used to stand outside the churches after Sunday Mass and hand out election literature for me with her father."

"As the years passed, how did your relationship with her father develop?"

"He is my principal organiser and supporter. He ensures that I always have enough backers in my local political organisation to guarantee that I receive sufficient support at election conventions to be re-nominated as a Dáil candidate. He has organised all my election campaigns."

"What can you tell the court about Colette's parents?"

"They are good people. Very attached to Colette. She is their only child. After her birth, her mother had some medical problem and was told she could never have another child. They are also devoutly religious people."

"How do you think they would have reacted if Colette had told them she was pregnant?"

Before Brannigan could reply, Paul Galloway was on his feet.

"That is a speculative question, judge. We know that Mr and Mrs James did not learn of Colette's pregnancy until some months after the child's birth. The witness should not be asked to speculate about how her parents would have reacted if they had been told of the pregnancy before the child's birth."

"Mr Galloway is right, Mrs Dell," responded Judge Flannery. "Whereas one might guess how Mr and Mrs James would have reacted to such distressing news, the witness cannot be asked to speculate under oath on this issue."

"I'm sorry, judge," Mrs Dell said. "I will approach the matter along another route. Are you still on good terms with Mr and Mrs James?" she asked Brannigan.

"I am."

"How frequently would Bill James contact you or you him?"

"We either meet or talk to each other by phone once or twice a week."

"When did Bill James learn of his daughter's pregnancy?"

"Not until some months after the baby was born." Brannigan's voice was trembling.

"Do you know how he learnt?"

"Sally Thomas, Colette's flatmate, told him."

"Do you know how he reacted?"

"He told me that when Colette called to the house he refused to let her in. He was very distressed, as was Margaret, his wife. On second thoughts 'distressed' would not fully describe his reaction. Devastated is, I think, a better word."

"How do you know this?"

"Because he contacted me the following day. Since then we have had endless discussions about Colette. After Colette's admission to hospital for a burst appendix, the family were reconciled. Colette now lives at home and her parents are supporting her in her attempt to recover custody of her child."

Paul Galloway wondered where Mrs Dell's questioning and Brannigan's evidence were leading. Evidence had already been given that Colette had concealed her pregnancy from her parents and about how they had reacted on hearing of Laura's birth. None of this had been disputed. It was also clear that Mr and Mrs James were sincere when they stated that if Laura was returned to their daughter she would live in their home and they would give every help necessary for her upbringing. Perhaps Mrs Dell thought that an additional witness confirming all this would assist her case. Galloway felt that nothing Brannigan had said so far would materially affect the evidence already given or would greatly influence any decision the judge might make.

"If Laura was returned to Colette James, do you believe her parents would give her every help?" asked Mrs Dell.

"I have no doubt that they would do so."

"I have no doubts about that either," interrupted Judge Flannery. "I don't think any questions have been raised about that, Mrs Dell."

The judge sounded impatient. Mrs Dell had deliberately painted the background picture of Brannigan's relationship with the James family before coming to the major part of his evidence. She realised that she had better get on with it now.

"Colette James is secretary to Michael O'Brien at present, is that correct?"

"Yes, she is."

"When she first went to work in Leinster House I understand that she was your secretary?"

"Yes, that's correct. She had left school and finished a secretarial course and her father was anxious that she get a job. My previous secretary transferred to work in a minister's office and Colette came to work for me."

"Colette was working for you when she became pregnant, is that right?"

"Yes, that's right."

"When did you learn of her pregnancy?"

"She told me about it the very day it was confirmed to her. This was approximately seven months before her baby was born."

"Do you know who the father of Colette's child is, Deputy Brannigan?"

"Yes, I do. I am," Brannigan replied in a monotone, audibly swallowing.

Paul Galloway now understood why Brannigan

was in the witness box. In her evidence, Colette had stated that she had initially worked for Brannigan, who was a friend of the family, and that following the birth of Laura she had gone to work for Michael O'Brien. Brannigan was the last TD in Leinster House that Galloway would have suspected of having fathered Laura. He had presumed that Colette had feigned sickness to Brannigan and so had not cross-examined her on the reason for her transferring to Michael O'Brien. Like Colette's parents, Galloway had thought that there was nothing unusual about Colette going to work for a young, newly elected TD, who needed help from an experienced Dáil secretary to learn the ropes.

Brannigan's admission that he was Laura's father had obviously startled Judge Flannery, who up to then had only been half-listening to what he had to say. It was clear to Paul Galloway that the judge had already decided that Brannigan's evidence was going to be of little value and that he had formed the view that Brannigan was merely in court as a friend of the family who meant well but who had little of substance to contribute.

"I beg your pardon, Deputy Brannigan, did I hear you correctly?" asked the judge. "You say you are the father of Miss James' child?"

"Yes, that's right, judge. I am the father."

Up until that moment Brannigan had given evidence without displaying much sign of emotion. He had lain awake in bed all night before phoning Robert Barnes and had mentally prepared himself for the courtroom ordeal. He now completely lost his nerve and felt compelled to explain, before Mrs Dell could ask another question, how he and Colette came to form their relationship. He turned to the judge.

"You see, judge, after Colette came to work for me, I realised she was no longer a gangly, freckled-faced young teenager but a very attractive young woman. I never wished her or her parents any harm. We became very close during those months. I never intended that this should happen . . . It's all my fault. I pretended to her that my marriage was virtually at an end and that I would get a church annulment and that we could marry. She believed me, but what I was saying was untrue. I took advantage of the situation. So I had to come to court. I could not conceal my involvement any longer."

Brannigan stopped. All the colour had drained from his face. Contrite and very upset, he slumped forward in the witness box and buried his head in his hands. There was total silence in the courtroom until the judge spoke.

"Take a glass of water, Deputy," said Judge Flannery, quickly recovering from the surprise caused by Brannigan's dramatic disclosure of paternity. "Would you like me to adjourn for a few minutes?" he asked Mrs Dell, who had remained standing, waiting for her witness to recover, before continuing with further questions. Before she could respond, Brannigan intervened.

"No, I'll be alright in a moment. I'm sorry," he said,

slowly lifting his head, breathing heavily and struggling to regain his composure.

The court registrar poured Brannigan a glass of water from the jug sitting on the table beside him. The politician slowly sipped from the glass, conscious that in the silent stillness of the courtroom he was the centre of attention. Feeling that he had regained control, he turned back to the judge.

"I'm sorry, judge . . . I think I'm ready to proceed," he said, though his voice faltered.

"Very well. If you're sure you're able for it, Mrs Dell may continue with her questions." The judge was impassive.

"For how long prior to Colette's pregnancy did you and she have a sexual relationship?" asked Mrs Dell.

"For approximately three months."

Brannigan told the story of his relationship with Colette, how their friendship had turned to intimacy and again how he had assured her that his marriage was at an end. It had been agreed between them that they would say nothing of their relationship to Colette's parents until after Brannigan had obtained a church annulment. Brannigan admitted that he had never sought an annulment and knew that he had no possibility of obtaining one. He described his reaction when Colette told him of her pregnancy and admitted that his wife and Colette's parents were still unaware of his relationship with her.

"How did Colette behave in the months leading up to Laura's birth?"

"In retrospect, her reaction was strange. She remained my secretary and continued to work for me. I wanted to avoid being drawn into discussions about the baby. Strangely, she also seemed to be anxious to avoid such discussions. When the subject came up, she simply told me that she would decide what to do when the baby was born. Although it did not strike me as odd then, I now believe that her behaviour was very peculiar."

"Why do you say that?"

"Well, the day she told me of her pregnancy I behaved very badly. My suggestion that she should consider . . . er . . . ending matters . . . I mean . . . having an abortion, clearly shocked and upset her greatly. Despite that, she returned to work three days later, calmly announcing she intended to remain working as my secretary and that she would make her own decisions about the baby. I was totally unnerved by the whole thing. She would come into work at ten every morning and finish at five in the evening as if nothing had happened. The only thing that changed was that she refused to work after five and I wasn't in a position to complain. I now believe that her behaviour at this time was unnatural. I think that she was in a permanent state of shock or in some sort of trance and that she just mechanically continued working through each day. Any other girl would have reacted with great emotion. You would have expected traumatic scenes and a great deal of upset. The whole thing was unreal. If I had not seen the way she carried on, I would not have believed that any girl of Colette's age, indeed any woman, could behave as she did in such circumstances. I had behaved appallingly. It was obvious that I had lied to her and misled her. Yet she never caused any rows, never threatened to tell my wife about our relationship, never, as far as I know, told other people in Leinster House of her predicament – that is, other than her flat-mate and Michael O'Brien, the TD she now works for. Her behaviour was just unnatural."

"Why do you think she behaved in this way?"

"It can only be because she was so shocked or numbed by what had happened, that she was in some way bottling it all up inside her and blocking it out of her mind. I even offered money to help with the medical expenses but she refused my offer and simply said that she would make her own arrangements and wanted nothing from me. I do not believe she was thinking clearly." Brannigan was now putting his point forcefully, anxious to ensure that the judge would accept his assessment of Colette's state of mind.

"Did she tell you she was arranging to have her baby adopted?"

"No, she never discussed it with me. Shortly after the child was born, she returned to work as Michael O'Brien's secretary and I guessed she had decided on adoption. I have not talked to Colette since the baby's birth. However, she returned to work so quickly that it was obvious she had decided on adoption. I was greatly relieved. I was scared stiff her attitude would change after the birth. It soon became clear to me, however, that she still had no wish to involve me further in what had happened. Whenever we passed by each other in Leinster House she would look away and pretend not to see me. Some months later when her father learned of the baby, he confirmed to me that it had been placed with adopters."

Brannigan's evidence continued. He described how he had deceived Bill James and pretended to know nothing about the baby or the identity of the father. With obvious discomfort, he described his meeting with Michael O'Brien and then went on to explain why he had decided to give evidence.

"I could not continue to hide from the truth. I realised that, apart from Sally Thomas, I was the only person who knew of Colette's pregnancy and saw her on a daily basis in the months preceding the birth of her baby – I mean our baby. I don't know how relevant it may be, but I felt it was important that the court be made aware of her behaviour during those months. I don't believe it was normal behaviour. At the time Colette gave her baby up for adoption she must have been under a great deal of stress and I'm not sure she truly knew what she was doing."

Mrs Dell sat down. It was two minutes to one on the courtroom clock. It was now Paul Galloway's turn to question Brannigan. Judge Flannery, seemingly not noticing the time, looked at Galloway expectantly as he rose from his seat.

"It's almost one o'clock, judge. Perhaps I shouldn't start until after lunch?" Galloway ventured.

"Oh, I'm very sorry, Mr Galloway," said the judge, glancing at the large wall clock. "I didn't realise it was so late. So be it. We shall resume at two o'clock, ladies and gentlemen."

As Judge Flannery stood and turned to walk out of the courtroom, Galloway felt relieved that he would have lunchtime to consider his line of cross-examination. It was clear that Brannigan had impressed the judge as being a truthful witness because he admitted his own despicable behaviour. He did not know to what extent the judge would accept that Colette's behaviour during the period of her pregnancy was unusual – so unusual as to support a conclusion that she was incapable of understanding what she was doing at the time when she placed Laura for adoption. Galloway realised that it was this part of Brannigan's evidence that was the most damaging. If he did not succeed in undermining it, the Mastersons could lose Laura.

twenty-four

Galloway had told the Mastersons that legal argument and submissions would take up the full day in court and could run into the following day. Neither they nor the biological mother could be present. John knew he would not be able to work and he did not want to leave Jenny on her own with Laura after they both had suffered another sleepless night. Neither John nor Jenny wished to spend the day in their Dublin home and, over breakfast, they decided to drive to Ashford. In case he needed to contact them, John phoned Galloway just before the solicitor left for court and gave him their Ashford cottage phone number as mobile phone coverage was not always reliable in the area. Then John, Jenny, Laura and Rebel piled into the car and drove into the beautiful Wicklow countryside. When they reached the Glen of the Downs, they called into the Glenview Hotel for morning tea and sandwiches and then continued on to their country cottage.

The weather was cold and John lit a blazing fire as Jenny searched in the freezer for some food that could be cooked for a late lunch. They spent a quiet day listening to music and playing games with Laura as Rebel fussed about the house on the trail of a fieldmouse. Jenny saw one run across the kitchen floor and disappear into a small hole in the timber wall. Rebel desperately stuck his nose into the hole, sniffing loudly, and then stood guard by it until the mouse sprinted by him and disappeared into a bedroom. Despite all his efforts and much to Jenny's relief, he failed to locate the little creature. She had no wish to be presented with a dead mouse by a triumphant Rebel.

After lunch, while Laura slept, John and Jenny lay on the giant six-foot bed that dominated their bedroom. John tenderly reached out to Jenny and wrapped her in his arms. Exhausted by the strain of the court case, their concern for Laura and their inability to sleep, they had not made love for almost two months. But now they gave passionate expression to their love for each other and felt the release of weeks of tension and pent-up emotion. Then, still holding each other tightly, they fell into an exhausted sleep.

* * *

It was just after nine in the morning when Colette awoke. Lying in bed with those heavy dark-brown curtains closing out the morning light, she relived the previous day's courtroom questioning. She could hear Galloway's hostile voice and her own muted response. She went over and over the replies she had given and knew that she would make a much better impression on the judge if she were only given a second chance. Why had she not explained herself better? Everything seemed fine when Mrs Dell questioned her, but the adopters' lawyer had confused her. It was so unfair. A court was supposed to get at the truth, but how could it when lawyers deliberately set out to prevent you telling your story properly, in your own way? Colette had told herself yesterday that what happened in the court no longer mattered but she now realised that it did matter. She had fooled herself into believing that even if the court case went against her she could still get Laura back. On the first day of the court hearing, instead of preparing herself for giving evidence, she had sat outside the courtroom in her car all day to follow the adopters to their home. She had planned not only to discover where they lived but had intended to return subsequently to kidnap Laura. If the judge wouldn't return Laura to her, she had decided she would get her back for herself.

Colette now realised that it was crazy even to entertain such thoughts. If she was caught, Laura would be taken from her and she could end up in prison. If she wasn't caught, she would have to remain on the run for the rest of her life because she couldn't return with Laura to her parents' home. She would have no home and no money. How could she even have considered such a wild scheme?

If only she had done better in the witness box!

Robert Barnes had told her that the entire day would be spent on legal argument. Barnes said he would phone her that night to advise her how the court case had gone and to tell her whether it was to continue into another day. She decided she would ask him when he phoned whether the judge would allow her to go into the witness box again. It was essential that the judge should understand how much she wanted Laura back. He would have to realise that, although Laura was too young to say what she wanted, if she were able to express an opinion she would say that she wanted to be with Colette – that she wanted to be with her real mother and her real grandparents. If only, thought Colette, she were allowed to sit in court to hear what was being said about her and about the adopters, and, more important, what was being said about Laura, her Laura, her daughter.

* * *

During the lunchtime adjournment, Paul Galloway read through the notes he had taken of the evidence given by Colette James the previous day, as well as his notes of Brannigan's evidence that morning. He had come to court that day mentally prepared for legal argument and had not expected to be engaging in further cross-examination. He knew that a clear recollection of Colette James' evidence was essential to enable him to question Brannigan properly, to identify and highlight the inconsistencies in what he had said and to undermine his credibility.

Galloway did not notice the time passing as he considered the approach he would adopt. In the end. Mrs Dell's return to the courtroom indicated that Judge Flannery would shortly resume. A few minutes later, all the lawyers having assembled and the judge again having taken his seat, Galloway rose to his feet as Seán Brannigan re-entered the witness box.

Galloway had decided to start with the most important issue of all. Brannigan's evidence had considerably strengthened the case being made that Colette James had not fully considered what she was doing when she had agreed to place Laura for adoption. Galloway had to attack that proposition.

"Deputy, am I right in saying that the only substantial discussion about the baby that took place between you and Miss James before its birth was on the day she revealed to you that she was pregnant?"

"I suppose that's correct."

"On that occasion you suggested to her that she have an abortion and she was so distressed by this suggestion that the discussion ended. Is that right?"

"Yes."

"And, despite the fact that she continued to work for you for a number of months, no further discussion took place between you before the baby's birth?"

"Other than my offering her some financial help with medical expenses . . ."

"An offer which she rejected?" interrupted Galloway.

"Yes."

"Could it not be that having seen your reaction and having recognised the reality of her predicament, Miss James decided on adoption at an early stage but had no wish to inform you of her decision?" Galloway was looking directly at the witness.

"I suppose that's possible." Brannigan nodded his head.

"Could that not adequately explain why there was so little recrimination on her part? Could that not explain her behaviour over those months?"

"Maybe," Brannigan replied, grim-faced.

"Did she ever suggest to you, during that time, that anyone was forcing her to have her baby adopted?"

"As I already said, she refused to discuss the baby with me after our unfortunate encounter . . . er . . . my unfortunate reaction when she told me about her pregnancy."

"You have had no discussions with her since the baby's birth?"

"I have not been in contact with her, although I have regularly talked to her father."

"Does Colette or her father know that you are giving evidence?"

"I don't know. I only contacted Mr Barnes this morning. I have not talked to any member of the

James family today. I don't know whether Mr Barnes has been in contact with them."

"At an earlier stage you were anxious to avoid involvement in court proceedings?"

"Yes, that's true."

"Why did you pay thirty-five thousand euro to Miss James' lawyers, Deputy?" asked Galloway.

"I was approached by Michael O'Brien, the Deputy Colette now works for. He told me that Colette was trying to get her daughter back but could not afford the legal fees that were involved."

"I think you sought certain assurances?" queried Galloway.

"I was anxious to ensure that . . . er . . . my . . . er . . . relationship with Colette would not become public knowledge. I was assured that Colette would tell no one I was the father of her child and that if she was successful in court, I would not be required to support the child."

"Why have you now come forward to give evidence?"

"Because of the almost daily reports from Bill James of Colette's difficulties; because I realise I cannot go on covering up my involvement. I cannot go on running away from the fact that I am Laura's father."

It was the first time Brannigan had referred to his daughter as "Laura" and not simply as Colette's "child" or "baby". Since the lunchtime adjournment, he had calmly and steadily answered all the questions put to him. He had steeled himself for the ordeal, erecting a barrier for his own emotional protection which he now pushed aside. Before Galloway could ask another question, Brannigan addressed the judge directly for the second time that day. He was angry now, resentful of the way Galloway harried him in the witness box.

"Judge, I am here to tell the truth. Colette's child is also my child, although for a long time I tried to ignore that this was so. Perhaps I am wrong about this, but I really believe that Colette's behaviour was not normal during the time she was pregnant. It might be my fault that she behaved the way she did. Before this court takes her daughter away from her permanently, I am anxious that everyone should understand the circumstances that gave rise to her placing Laura for adoption. I also want the court to know that if Laura is returned to Colette, I will give Colette any financial help she requires to enable her to bring up and educate our daughter. I will do anything I can to help her . . . anything . . ."

Brannigan's voice trailed off. He turned his head and stared defiantly at Galloway as if daring him to ask more questions. Galloway held his ground momentarily and stared back. He then turned to Judge Flannery and announced that he had no further questions to put to the witness.

twenty-five

"I don't believe you," Colette James exclaimed excitedly as Robert Barnes described the day's events to her over the phone.

"Well, that's what happened. Paul Galloway cross-examined him until about three thirty and when he finished the judge adjourned the court until eleven o'clock tomorrow morning. We will then definitely be into legal argument."

"And what do you think now?" Colette asked expectantly.

"Brannigan's evidence certainly did you no harm. I know you'd like me to do so, but I cannot predict what conclusion the judge will reach or what decision he will make. Brannigan's description of his own behaviour and the way he deceived you must, I believe, have some influence on him. I just don't know to what extent it will influence his final decision."

"Surely it will persuade the judge that Laura should be returned to me!"

"It will help our case. I have little doubt about that." Barnes was anxious to give Colette some encouragement and reassurance.

"Is there nothing more I can do? Could I go back into the witness box? I'm sure that if I was given another opportunity to do so, I could convince the judge that Laura should be returned to me," Colette said pleadingly.

"I'm afraid that's not possible," Barnes gently responded. "Just as the adopters can't go back into the witness box and repeat their evidence, the judge would not allow you to do so either."

"But I was so nervous yesterday. I am sure I didn't properly explain to him what happened or why I want Laura back. It's all such a blur. If I had another chance I know I could make him understand . . ." Colette's voice trailed off.

* * *

"Oh no, not another day," was Jenny's response when she heard Galloway's news that the case had not yet finished.

The phone had been ringing as they opened the front door of their cottage in Ashford and Jenny had gone to answer it. They were returning after taking Laura for a late afternoon walk in her buggy.

"Another witness? I thought all the evidence on

the mother's side had concluded yesterday!" she exclaimed.

"Well, Laura's biological father came forward unexpectedly to give evidence today. I can't tell you who he is because the court has ordered that his identity should not be revealed so as to preserve everyone's anonymity. All I can tell you about him is that he is a TD and married and that he has concealed his relationship with the mother from his wife and his family. In his evidence he described his reaction when she told him that she was pregnant and he gave an account of their relationship up to the time when Laura was placed for adoption."

"I see," said Jenny, breaking out in a cold sweat. She leaned against the wall beside the phone and forced herself to speak. "Has his coming forward helped the mother? What effect will his evidence have?"

"I don't know. I believe he was of some help to the mother's case in so far as he confirmed that he had behaved badly towards her and had misled not only his own family but also her family by concealing the fact that he was Laura's father. I think his evidence may also make the judge a bit more sympathetically disposed towards the mother. However, much of what he said just confirmed what the court already knew. In a nutshell, he has made our case a little bit more difficult, but I would not get unduly pessimistic." Galloway fully understood the impact of what he was saying on Jenny.

"Will there be any more witnesses tomorrow?" Jenny asked wearily.

"Not as far as I know. The legal argument should finally start tomorrow. It may finish by the afternoon or could continue into the following morning. Either way, the judge will reserve his judgement and it could be some weeks before he delivers his decision. I'll phone you again tomorrow about this time."

twenty-six

Once again they were all assembled in the Ó'Dálaigh House courtroom. The dramatic evidence of the previous day now seemed less relevant and less important to Paul Galloway. On reflection, he thought that the unexpected admission of paternity by Brannigan had not added greatly to the mother's case. She had decided on adoption at an early stage before the birth of her child and had been counselled by the social worker, Mrs Comerford, who had urged her not to make a hasty decision. Despite the social worker's counselling, she had insisted on signing the adoption papers when Laura was only five days old and the consequences of her doing so had been fully and properly explained to her. Galloway knew that if the judge accepted this interpretation of the mother's conduct he would rule that her agreement to place

Laura for adoption was valid. He then had to be persuaded that the child's best interests required that an adoption order be made. Galloway knew that if he failed to convince the judge of the validity of the adoption agreement his clients were in serious trouble.

Judge Flannery spoke first.

"Mr Galloway, since the adopters were heard in evidence first, you are to commence the legal submissions."

"As you please," responded Galloway, dutifully rising to his feet.

He started by outlining to the court a brief history of the events that had led up to Colette James placing her child for adoption, and then began legal argument.

"For the adopters to succeed, the court must be satisfied that Colette James truly agreed to the placing of her child, Laura, for adoption and that it is in the best interests of the child that the Adoption Authority be empowered to dispense with the need for Miss James' consent so that an adoption order can be made. In 1978 the former Chief Justice, O'Higgins C.J., stated in the Supreme Court that a valid agreement to place requires 'a free consent on the part of the mother given in full knowledge of the consequences which follow upon her placing her child for adoption' (see *G versus An Bord Uchtála*). There is, in my submission, no doubt that the social worker, Mrs Comerford, explained the full implications and legal consequences of what she was doing to the mother and that the mother understood them. She admitted so in her own evidence. The mother chose to conceal her pregnancy from her parents and deliberately decided not to discuss her plans with the father of her child. Having considered her own circumstances and the various options available to her well before the birth of her child, she decided to place her baby for adoption. The fact that she might have made a different decision in different circumstances, or the fact that she subsequently developed doubts and eventually changed her mind, does not, in my respectful submission, alter the position. She herself decided on adoption and she gave her agreement voluntarily, fully appreciating what she was doing.

Galloway paused, observing that the judge was taking detailed notes of what he was saying. He waited until the judicial pen had stopped writing and then continued.

"Having signed the adoption agreement, the mother knew and understood the adoption process had commenced and she has admitted that this is so. She expressly rejected the social worker's suggestion that she should see her baby again before signing the adoption papers, or that the baby should be placed for some weeks in foster care so that the mother might give some further consideration to her position. It is, accordingly, my submission that there can be no doubt as to the validity of the mother's agreement to place the child, Laura, for adoption."

Galloway hesitated, again waiting for the judge to stop writing. A few seconds later Judge Flannery looked up.

"Please continue, Mr Galloway."

"Certainly, judge. I now turn to the issue of the best interests of the child. It is generally accepted that the child is living in a stable, caring household and has become a member of the adopters' family in the fullest sense. She is happy and well-adjusted and developing normally. In her evidence Dr O'Connell was unequivocal that the best interests of the child lay with her remaining with the adopters. Dr Lloyd was more circumspect. Nevertheless, both child psychiatrists acknowledged that the child was doing well with the adopters, that she had no relationship at all with the biological mother and that being transferred to the mother's custody would cause considerable suffering to the child and would retard her development. Dr O'Connell also stated that such transference would cause long-term harm and could permanently damage Laura's development. Dr Lloyd also acknowledged this possibility."

Galloway paused, his eyes fixed on the judge's pen, waiting for him to look up – the signal that he could continue. He was anxious to ensure that the judge fully transcribed all the points he was making. The writing stopped and Galloway resumed.

"The child Laura does not know her biological mother and has no relationship with her. She has bonded with and formed attachments to the adopters, who are in fact Laura's psychological parents. She has also formed a series of attachments to relatives and friends of the adopters. In my submission, the only conclusion consistent with Laura's best interest is that she be permitted to remain with the adopters and that her *factual* relationship with them be made legally permanent. Accordingly, the Adoption Authority should, judge, be empowered to dispense with the need for the biological mother's consent to the making of the adoption order."

Galloway stopped speaking and there was a momentary silence in the courtroom, all eyes concentrating on the judge as he continued to note down what had been said.

Galloway then concluded: "I do not think there is anything further I can add at this stage. I don't know, judge, whether there are any questions you may wish to raise?"

He remained standing, waiting for the judicial response.

"I don't think so," replied the judge. "There is nothing I want to put to you at this stage, Mr Galloway. I will wait to hear what Mrs Dell has to say."

"Very well, judge," replied Galloway as he slowly sat down. Glancing at his watch he realised that he had been on his feet for less than one hour. He had expected it to take longer. He had anticipated that the judge would raise a number of questions with him during the course of his submission and was surprised that he had not done so. He did not know whether the fact the judge had not put points to him augured well or not. Judge Flannery had silently taken notes throughout his submission. Could it be, Galloway wondered, that he was going to rely on those notes to make a decision in favour of the Mastersons, or was it that he had already decided in favour of the mother?

Judge Flannery looked towards Mrs Dell.

"Mrs Dell, do you wish to proceed?"

"I do, judge. I believe no submissions are to be made on behalf of the Adoption Authority," she responded, rising from her seat.

"That is so," said Adrian Owen. "As regards the dispute between the adopters and the biological mother, the Authority is strictly neutral and does not take sides."

"Very well, Mrs Dell, proceed," instructed the judge.

"Like my friend, Mr Galloway. I shall first address you, judge, on the issue of the validity of Miss James' agreement to place Laura for adoption and thereafter deal with the issue of where Laura's best interests lie."

Mrs Dell first sketched in the background and, unlike Galloway, emphasised Colette James' youth, her general inexperience of life and her sexual inexperience, the manner in which she had been deceived by Brannigan (a person whom she had trusted and admired since childhood) and her fears as to how her parents would react if they learnt of her relationship with Brannigan and especially if they found out about her pregnancy.

Turning to legal argument, she continued: "For an adoption agreement to be valid, the mother's consent to placement must be given freely with full knowledge of the consequences and circumstances and neither the advice of others involved in the adoption process nor the surrounding circumstances should deprive the mother of the capacity to make a fully informed free decision. In the words of Mr Justice Walsh in the Supreme Court (see *G versus An Bord Uchtála*) 'a consent motivated by fear, stress, anxiety or dictated by poverty or other deprivation does not constitute a valid consent'. According to Colette James' own evidence, she was in a state of shock upon learning that she was pregnant.

"The psychological impact of her pregnancy on Colette was compounded and exacerbated by the appalling reaction by the father of her child to the news of her pregnancy. A man she had known for years, and who had held out to her a promise of matrimony, abandoned her to her fate on the very day she went to him for help. This girl who had lived with her parents all her life, felt that she had no alternative but to move out of her home into a friend's flat to conceal her pregnancy from them. She lived in fear that they would learn of it and for most of her pregnancy had no choice but to continue to work for the father of her child so as to maintain an income, although she clearly felt abandoned and rejected by him.

"When Miss James was in hospital for the birth of her child, she deluded herself into believing that she was recovering from an illness and not from childbirth. She cut herself off from reality so much that she even refused to see her baby on the day after she was born. She only named the child when she was cajoled into doing so by the hospital registrar. It wasn't until months later, when she visited the home of Michael O'Brien's sister and saw her feeding a baby some weeks younger than her own, that the enormity of what had happened in her life finally dawned on her and she confronted reality. It is my submission, judge, that Colette James never freely and knowingly agreed to her child being placed for adoption. Her actions were motivated by stress and anxiety and were dominated by a fear of being permanently alienated from and rejected by her parents, a not unrealistic terror when viewed against their initial reaction to the news of the birth of their grandchild. It is my submission that during this period in her young life, Colette James cut herself off from reality and was not rationally able to assess her position and make a considered decision about her child's future. Moreover, while the social worker, Mrs Comerford, showed Miss James every kindness, there was one flaw in her approach. Though she did suggest to her that her baby could be temporarily placed in foster care to give Miss James more time to consider her position, she did not propose to her that Laura be placed in a children's home as an alternative to adoption. Thus all of the available options were not discussed with Colette James before her child was handed over to the adopters."

Like Galloway before her, Mrs Dell hesitated to allow the judge time to complete the note he was taking. A few moments later he looked up and she continued.

"It is not difficult to imagine the anxious and troubled state of mind of this lonely girl, who, living away from home, unknown to her family had given birth to a child outside of marriage. Secrecy had to be maintained at all costs. It is my submission that at the time when her child, Laura, was given by her to the adoption society, her judgement was so impaired and she was under such strain as to render her legally incapable of entering into a valid agreement for the adoption of her child."

Mrs Dell paused for breath. Judge Flannery stopped writing and looked at the clock. It was almost lunchtime.

"I think we'll stop now for lunch, Mrs Dell. I am sure everyone will be glad of a breather. These are most distressing cases. I will resume at two fifteen sharp."

Judge Flannery rose and bowed to the lawyers assembled in the courtroom. They all stood in silence as he walked into the judges' chamber at the back of the courtroom, closing the door behind him. He was obviously troubled.

twenty-seven

At two fifteen the court hearing resumed. Mrs Dell stood up and continued her submissions.

"Before lunch I submitted, judge, that the mother's agreement to place the child, Laura, for adoption is invalid. If that is so, this court cannot provide for her adoption. If you do not hold with me on that matter, you must then consider whether it is in the best interests of the child that the court permit an adoption order to be made. I shall now turn to this issue.

"Mr Justice Kenny in the Supreme Court has emphasised the importance of the blood relation between mother and child. The blood link, he stated, means that an instinctual understanding will exist between mother and child which will not be there if a child remains with adopters (see *G versus An Bord Uchtála*). Much has been made of the evidence that the adopters are the child's psychological parents. That is so because the mother has not had an opportunity to parent her child.

"It has become fashionable to regard a child's relationship with its psychological parents as more important than its relationship by blood with its real mother. However, for centuries our courts have emphasised the importance of the blood link and it is my respectful submission that the evidence heard in this case is not sufficient to override the views expressed by Mr Justice Kenny. Laura is Colette James' own flesh and blood. She was carried by her for nine months of pregnancy. This important link between mother and child cannot be ignored."

Mrs Dell waited a moment, anxious to ensure that the judge was following her reasoning. He was engrossed in taking notes. As he looked up and nodded in her direction, she resumed. Galloway, who was observing the proceedings closely was uncertain whether the nod simply indicated that she should continue or whether Judge Flannery was agreeing with what Mrs Dell had said.

"In his evidence Dr Lloyd stated that there was no reason why Laura could not form new bonds and attachments with her biological mother if she were returned to her. It is my submission that it is in the best interest of the child that she be allowed to develop such bonds with her real mother and that she should not be deprived of the right and opportunity to do so.

"In a similar case in 1984 where a baby had been in the care of adopters for ten months, the High Court ordered that the baby be returned to its mother. In the case Mr Justice O'Hanlon stated that he could 'not help feeling that a baby and growing child would always be better off with its biological mother if she is a devoted and concerned parent and can provide in a reasonable manner for the physical as well as emotional needs of the child'. Colette James is such a mother and, with the assistance of her parents, Laura's grandparents, she can fully and comprehensively provide for her daughter's physical and emotional needs."

"Mrs Dell, could you address me on an issue I raised in the course of the evidence?" interrupted Judge Flannery. "That is, the issue of the child's best interests if some years after her adoption she tried to find her roots and discovers her biological mother's identity and, in doing so, learns that she was legally adopted only as a result of a court contest between the adopters and her mother."

"Certainly, judge. I was about to come to that issue. In her evidence Dr O'Connell stated that if the child was permanently removed from the adopters her removal could result in serious psychological repercussions in later life. It is my submission that this aspect of her evidence should not be accepted by the court. It is a matter about which the psychiatrists disagree. It is not so much factual evidence as predictive evidence which involves gazing into a psychological crystal ball in an attempt to predict the future. It could equally well be predicted that if Laura learns in later years that the adopters defeated her mother in a court battle in order to adopt her and deprived her mother of the opportunity of bringing her up, such information could have a devastating psychological impact with far-reaching consequences. This is a matter that should be seriously considered in determining what course of action is in the child's best interests. In my submission this hypothesis at the very least is of equal validity to the predictions made by Dr O'Connell.

"Finally, judge, it is my submission that the only course of action consistent with the best interests and welfare of the child Laura is that she be returned to the custody of her biological mother. Even if you hold that adoption agreement to be valid, you may still refuse to permit the child's adoption and order that she be returned to the custody and care of her mother. I ask you that you so order."

Mrs Dell sat down.

"Thank you, Mrs Dell," said Judge Flannery. "Mr Galloway, do you wish to reply now or should we adjourn until tomorrow morning? I am willing to sit late this afternoon if necessary."

Galloway was anxious to minimise the impact of Mrs Dell's well-argued submission, which, he suspected, might have had a considerable influence on Judge Flannery. He did not want the judge to go home that night with his thoughts burdened by the tragic picture of the plight of Colette James so vividly and powerfully portrayed by her articulate counsel. He wanted to ensure that the judge's sympathies also extended to the situation of Jenny and John Masterson and even more so to that of Laura.

"I am in a position to reply now, judge, if you so wish," Galloway quickly responded, rising to his feet. "I should be able to complete matters within an hour."

"Very well," said the judge. "Proceed."

"Judge, I do not intend to cover again the ground dealt with in my initial submissions. I shall, however, reply to Mrs Dell's submissions by first dealing with the adoption agreement and then consider the child's best interests.

"With regard to the adoption agreement the case is made that the mother was so distressed that she didn't really know what she was doing and, consequently, did not voluntarily agree to her child's adoption. It is my submission that the pressures felt by the mother were no different from those experienced by most mothers who place their children for adoption. She had been made fully aware of the consequences of her actions and she wanted to have her child adopted. In the words of Mr Justice McWilliam 'the court must consider these issues from a practical point of view'. The learned judge emphasised that the mere fact of having a child outside marriage 'causes stress and anxiety' and 'if absolute rules as to fear, stress, anxiety or poverty were to be applied there could hardly be a case found in which one or other of them would not be present' so that it could be argued that an adoption agreement was not valid. It is my submission that all the evidence heard in this case is consistent with the view that the mother made a deliberate and considered decision to have her child adopted. In the circumstances, her agreement to adopt must be valid. If this mother's agreement is held to be invalid, all future adoption agreements, except those signed by the most cold-hearted mothers, would be put at risk of being overturned at a later date.

"As to the child's best interest and the importance Mrs Dell attaches to the blood relationship between the child and the biological mother, this case must decide upon the evidence as heard by the court. No strong or serious support was given by either psychiatrist to the importance of the blood link as a feature in the future welfare of Laura. Both psychiatrists agreed, however, that it would have a traumatic impact on Laura, at least in the short term, if she were taken from the home of the adopters. The evidence in this case presents two options: the first option is to permit Laura to remain in the custody of the adopters whom she loves as parents, with whom she is developing normally, and to allow her to retain and build on bonds and attachments that she has formed not only with the adopters but also with their extended family; the second option is to transfer Laura to the custody of a parent she does not know and who even had difficulties in coping with her in the brief meeting that took place at St Mark's, to terminate her relationship with all the people she has known since her birth, to cause her to suffer immediate distress and serious disruption in her development, and to place her at serious risk of long-term psychological harm. It is my submission that the decision consistent with Laura's best interest is the one that embraces the former option. As for the possibility of her reacting adversely in later years upon learning of the circumstances of her adoption, this is a matter of speculation or conjecture. No evidence of substance has been given to support this theory. It is not, therefore, something that should in any way influence the court in the determination that has to be made.

"Finally, Mrs Dell referred to a case in which Justice O'Hanlon ordered the return to a biological mother of a child who had been in the care of adopters for ten months. She omitted to mention that in that case the learned judge acknowledged that 'if too long a period is allowed to elapse before the return of the child from the adoptive parents is sought the bonds of attachment between the child and the psychological parents may have been so strongly formed as to be incapable of being broken without lasting damage to the child's personality'. The child Laura has been in the care of the adopters for over fourteen months and it is my submission that her bonds of attachment are by now very strongly formed. In no adoption case of this nature to date have our courts returned a child to a biological mother where the child has been in the care of the adopters for more than twelve months."

"Is that so, Mr Galloway?" queried the judge. "Am I not right in saying that much older children have been returned to biological parents in other cases?"

"That is so, judge, but only in circumstances where there has been a married couple seeking the return to them of a child placed for adoption by the mother before her marriage to the child's father. There is no prospect in this case, as we have heard, of the mother marrying the father of her child," replied Galloway, knowing that the judge had been researching court decisions during the course of the lengthy court hearing.

"Yes, that is true, you are correct in that," responded the judge. "However, am I also not correct in stating that, while the courts have in previous decisions returned to their mothers children who have been with adopters for no more than twelve months and have allowed the adoption of children who have been with adopters for sixteen months or longer, *no* decision has yet been delivered in respect of a child who has been with adopters for more than twelve months but less than sixteen months? Since the child Laura has been with the Mastersons for just fourteen months, are we not in this case dealing with uncharted territory?"

"That is so to some extent, judge, save that the psychiatric evidence in this instance is more consistent with that supplied in the cases in which the adopters have been successful than with that given in the cases in which biological mothers have been successful."

Galloway hesitated to see whether any further judicial questions would arise.

"Thank you, Mr Galloway. Is there anything further you wish to add?" asked Judge Flannery.

Galloway considered for a moment. Was there anything further he should say? Had he adequately responded to Mrs Dell's comprehensive submissions and fully answered the judge's probing questions? There is always a doubt. A temptation to go back over issues already dealt with. A fear that if you do so, you may irritate the judge; a worry that if you do not, the judge might pay insufficient attention to something that could be crucial in determining the result.

"Is that all, Mr Galloway?" enquired the judge breaking the silence.

Galloway knew there was nothing new he could add.

"It is, judge. I will conclude by submitting to you that all of the evidence persuasively indicates that it is in the best interest of the child Laura that she be adopted by Jenny and John Masterson."

He sat down, relieved that the court hearing had at length concluded. There was nothing more he could do now. There was nothing more to be said.

The assembled lawyers looked up at the judge, who was thoughtfully turning the pages of his notebook. He then addressed them all.

"These cases impose an intolerable burden on everyone involved – on the parties to the proceedings, in this case the Mastersons and Miss James, on their families, their lawyers and also on the judge. I wish to thank you all for the conscientious way in which you have presented and argued this most difficult and disturbing case before me. Whatever decision I make is going to cause heartbreak and distress to some of those involved. I will not unduly add to everyone's anxiety by unnecessarily delaying my decision. The burden of giving judgement now falls upon my shoulders. I shall deliver my judgement at 10.30 a.m. this day week."

Judge Flannery stood up and rapidly walked out of the courtroom.

Mrs Dell turned to Galloway.

"Well argued. You did everything you could for your clients."

"You did too. It's been a hell of a fight. What way do you think it will go?"

"I don't know. I just don't know," replied Mrs Dell wearily.

"Well, we'll know this day week," Galloway said quietly as he bent over the table to gather together the various law reports he had scattered across it when delivering his legal submissions.

twenty-eight

"It's over," John announced to Jenny as he walked into the kitchen. "Paul Galloway said the court sat until five this afternoon. The judge is giving his decision next Thursday at ten thirty in the morning."

"How did he say it went today?" asked Jenny anxiously.

"He said things went as well as could be expected. He didn't go into much detail and he's still being very cautious."

"I wish we could have at least been there. What harm could have been done by our listening to the lawyers? It's all about Laura. The judge's decision is going to affect all of us. It is going to determine her future, our future. Oh, John, the last few days have been such hell. If we had been allowed to be there and listen it would have made them that bit more bearable."

"I know. I wish we could have been there too," John replied in an exhausted whisper.

They had been over it so many times. Jenny sat down morosely at the kitchen table. During the days of the court hearing she had fought successfully to control her emotions. She knew John was fighting a similar battle and that his external composure masked a pain and turmoil no different from her own. He sat down beside her and they silently embraced. Each knew and understood the fears of the other, neither needed to put words to that fear. It was better that it remain unspoken. They now only had a week to wait and then they would know. There was nothing more they could do. Now it all depended on the judge. Seven days had to pass and they had to live each of those days to the full. The only thing that was certain in their lives was that for all of those seven days Laura would remain in their home. Both John and Jenny knew that, even if the judge was to order that Laura be taken from them, she would always be a part of them. They would never forget her and their love for her would never be extinguished.

*　*　*

Colette felt totally alone. There was no one she felt she could fully confide in or rely on. Michael O'Brien had been supportive and helpful, but there was no real intimacy between them. The court case was over and he had to get on with his own life.

Sally Thomas had been a good friend during the months they had lived together but since Colette had returned home they had grown apart and were seeing less of each other. She suspected that Sally's visits to her were more out of sympathy than out of friendship.

Colette thought that the reconciliation with her parents after her hospitalisation had been complete, but she now knew that her relationship with them was fragile and had been further damaged by Seán Brannigan's visit to her home. This occurred shortly after Barnes' phone call to her the previous evening telling her of Brannigan's appearance as a surprise witness on her behalf. The initial elation aroused by his coming forward had been quickly dampened by the reaction of her parents to Brannigan's revelations about their relationship and of his paternity of Laura. The love and trust that had been rebuilt in the weeks following her return from hospital were superseded by a new anger and resentment in her parents.

"Why didn't you tell us?" her father had asked bitterly after Brannigan had left. "Why didn't you confide in us? Why did we have to hear it from him?"

"I just couldn't tell you. I just couldn't!" she had replied helplessly, tears streaming down her cheeks.

Colette had fled to the bedroom to escape any further discussion, to give her parents some time to come to terms with what Brannigan had told them. She hoped they would eventually understand but did not expect that they would and felt a new gulf had opened up between them.

Lying on her bed, Colette thought of Laura. She remembered the thick blonde hair and the beautiful bright blue eyes that had stared at her when they had played the biscuit game in St Mark's. No longer had she to struggle to recall her looks. She could see the sparkle in her daughter's eyes and knew that she was beautiful. She knew that she loved her and that she would always love her. Without her she would remain alone for ever.

twenty-nine

Brian Flannery was sixty-two years of age. He was a legal scholar and after five years working as a young barrister, a junior counsel, he had established a reputation as an able and powerful advocate and was recognised as a rapidly rising star within the Irish legal profession. While his legal contemporaries still retained their junior rank, at the young age of twenty-nine he had taken silk and had become a senior counsel. In his twenty years at the senior bar he was reputed to have earned vast sums of money in controversial and highly publicised trials. On his fiftieth birthday he had been elevated to the bench and his appointment as a judge of the High Court had been widely welcomed. His twelve years as a member of the judiciary had enhanced his reputation. His capacity to adjudicate fairly and incisively upon complex legal controversies gained him widespread respect and admiration not only among lawyers but also among the general public.

As he walked the length of Dun Laoghaire pier on that sunny Sunday afternoon in March, Judge Brian Flannery was troubled. An avuncular man unaffected by the trappings of office, he normally returned the friendly greetings and nods of recognition from passers-by as he undertook his only regular weekly exercise. This Sunday, his mind elsewhere, greetings and nods went unacknowledged.

Twice during that weekend he had sat down to write the judgement he was to deliver the following Thursday. Despite his years as a judge, this was only the third occasion on which he had to deliver judgement in an adoption dispute. Both of the earlier cases had been comparatively straightforward. In the first, he had ordered at the conclusion of the court hearing that a child who had been with adopters for five months should be returned to the biological mother. In the second case he had ordered that two young children aged seven and nine, a brother and sister, should remain with adopters with whom they had lived for over six years. Although their mother refused to consent to an adoption order being made, she did not want her children back and had failed even to appear in court to give evidence.

These two cases had been simple and the decisions to be made were obvious. The Masterson and James case was so terribly different.

At the end of the dramatic four-day courtroom

battle over Laura, Judge Flannery was still unsure of his decision. He had spent all Friday reading through his notes of the evidence and the conflicting legal submissions he had heard. On the Saturday morning, although still uncertain of his decision, he had written a judgement favouring the Mastersons. The completion of the judgement had not dispelled his doubts and uncertainty. A visit to his daughter, her husband and their one-year-old son, his only grandchild, that Saturday afternoon, added to his feeling of unease. As he watched mother and child play together he thought of the heartache his decision would cause Colette James and recalled the pain in her voice when she was giving evidence. Could it really be true that this young child Laura had no relationship with her mother, he wondered. If it was true, would such a relationship not grow rapidly if mother and child were together? For decades the courts would have taken such a view. Modern psychiatry had convinced many of his judicial colleagues of another view: that the psychological link between a child and the people parenting it was of more importance than its biological link to its biological parent, its own flesh and blood. Was this a valid approach? Could the psychiatrists and psychologists be relied upon?

Brian Flannery's judgement in favour of the Mastersons deeply troubled him. That Sunday morning he had sat down and written a second judgement, this time in favour of Colette James. He had then read through both judgements and was still unsure.

He stood and watched the waves lash against the boulders along the side of the pier and went over both judgements in his mind. He thought of the child Laura. How curious it was that he had to decide the future of a child whom he had never seen and who he would never meet but who had been fought over for four days in his court. The decision he made would have a profound effect on her life and on the lives of all of those close to her, yet he would never know whether the decision he must make would ultimately prove right or wrong.

As he turned to walk back down the pier, he pondered on the fact that he had written two judgements, either of which would cause joy and grief, but that he still did not know which judgement he would deliver. He had to make his decision according to the law, but the law gave him only limited guidance. Only he could decide whether Colette James had fully and clearly agreed to her daughter being placed for adoption, or whether it was in Laura's best interests that she be returned to her mother or remain with the adopters. He had to decide the future for them all.

Conscious of the enormity of the decision he had to make, Brian Flannery again turned over in his mind what the various witnesses had said during the course of the four-day hearing.

Later that evening as he knelt in church praying for guidance, he knew that by Thursday morning he would have to make his decision. He had to play God but God could not help him. To deliver judgement was his duty and the consequences of his judgement would be his responsibility. He alone had to decide with whom Laura should spend the rest of her childhood and no one could help him determine which side his judgement should favour.

thirty

It was three o'clock and it was Friday. The bell rang and within a few seconds children started pouring out of the school gates, some on bicycles, some running, some walking. Parents waving arms, dogs excitedly barking and car horns blaring to attract attention all added to the chaos that quickly developed outside the school grounds.

The day was hot, unexpectedly so, considering the time of year. The growing line of green-uniformed teenagers stretched out along the path from the bus stop looking from a distance like a giant expanding green caterpillar. Talk of pop stars, websites, hockey matches, television serials and football heroes travelled through the air in a confused cacophony. Four schoolboys, unseen by the supervising teacher surveying the scene from the school gates, hid behind a large oak tree that rose majestically out of the ground three hundred yards beyond the school, waiting to jump out behind the three attractive fifteen-year-old girls who were slowly making their way to the bus stop, engrossed in conversation.

The girls were within ten feet of the tree when, giggling, they broke into a sprint and ran past the startled boys, who up until that moment had believed themselves to be invisible.

"Hey, wait!" the red-haired boy with freckles called out. "Wait for us!"

They rushed after the girls, who greeted them with laughter and jeers.

"You thought we couldn't see you, you thought we couldn't see you!" the girls chorused playfully.

"Okay, so you spotted us. Big deal," responded the freckled boy, looking crestfallen.

"Oh, don't take it so seriously," responded the blue-eyed girl with long blonde hair, giving him a friendly hug. "We're only teasing."

Talking of the coming weekend, they continued their walk along the path together as traffic sped by them. The school junior hockey finals were being played on Saturday and the girls were all members of the team. It was the first time the school had reached the final and they had been bubbling over with excitement all week. The teachers had noticed the unusual restlessness in class and the air of expectation that hung over the school. As the week drew to a close, the likely outcome of the final had become the only serious topic of discussion for everyone – pupils and teachers alike. The whole school would turn out tomorrow and all eyes would be on the eleven girls of the school team as they took to the pitch.

They had almost reached the bus stop and were no longer within sight of the supervising teacher. The red-haired boy called Dónal and the blonde girl discreetly held hands as they turned the corner and then broke into a trot together, reaching the bus stop just ahead of the double-decker bus racing towards them. Outstretched hands brought the bus to a halt and they all clambered aboard and went upstairs.

Talk of tomorrow's match centred on whether the blonde girl would score again. She had scored in every cup match played so far in the school's cup games. The bus ground to a halt to let passengers on and off and the boys and girls, locked in conversation, were cheerfully oblivious of the newspaper posters which stood against newspaper stalls along the bus route carrying the early evening's main headlines.

SEÁN BRANNIGAN, TD FOR THIRTY YEARS, DIES, the *Evening Herald* solemnly proclaimed.

AN TAOISEACH, MICHAEL O'BRIEN, SAD AT DEATH OF LONG-SERVING TD, the *Evening Press* long-windedly announced.

The political events of the day did not distract the home-going travellers on the bus from their animated discussion of the following day's hockey final.

* * *

Saturday arrived and the weather remained exceptional for early April. The sun shone brightly and no clouds lingered in the light blue sky. She had followed Liffey Valley, Ireland's leading women's hockey team, for over five years, ever since she had been first taken to watch the team play and had often imagined what it would be like one day to play on their famous hockey pitch to the cheers and applause of spectators sitting in the modern stadium. She had hoped to play there when she was older, hoped to join the famous club and play for them and perhaps one day play for Leinster and maybe even for Ireland. Never had she imagined that she would have the opportunity to play on the famous pitch so soon.

She knew she was nervous and, as she changed, she felt the same butterflies in her stomach that had accompanied her to the dressing room when they had been competing against other school teams in earlier rounds of the cup competition. Her friend, Patricia, who played in goal, had been chattering away to her incoherently for almost five minutes, making no sense at all. She ignored what was being said to her and concentrated on what she had to do. Although she had tried to convince herself during the previous few days that this game was no different to the others she had played, she did not truly believe that. Since she was the goal-scorer, she knew that if the school team was to win she had to score.

A welcoming roar of school and parental support greeted their arrival onto the hockey pitch. She had disciplined herself to ignore the noise, concentrate on the game and not to be distracted. A second roar announced the arrival of the opposing team. Coins tossed, ends decided, a whistle blew and the match started. Her school instantly attacked, putting the opposition on the defensive and she ran for goal. Suddenly she was inside the circle and the ball was at her feet. She drew back her hockey stick and hit it with all her strength. Transfixed, she watched the ball hit the roof of the net. She had never before scored with her very first strike. A deafening roar greeted the goal and she was smothered in hugs and kisses from the rest of the team. The referee's whistle cut short the celebrations and called the players back to the centre circle for the game to restart. As she ran back, she permitted herself for the first time to look up into the stand and to wave.

John and Jenny Masterson, yelling with excitement, jumped up and down and cheered their daughter's achievement. They'd had a premonition that she would score. It was on this date exactly fourteen years ago that they had won the right to adopt Laura and now they and Laura would in the future have their own special reason to celebrate this day. Together they rejoiced in and celebrated both their own and Laura's success. They now did not doubt that not only would her school team win the cup but that Laura would go on to fulfil her ambition and play hockey for Ireland.

Unseen by John or Jenny Masterson or by Laura, in the far corner of the ground a solitary blonde figure stood, worn down by years of heartache and remorse, eyes glistening, staring in admiration at the attractive athletic teenage hockey player who had so brilliantly scored and to whom she bore a curious resemblance. The whistle blew and the game restarted. She continued to stand and watch. Colette James wondered how she should respond if the blonde girl should again score and by some accident or miracle turn and wave to her.